ONE OF THE GUYS

A.R. PERRY

LEGENDARY BOOKS

Legendary Books

One of the Guys

A.R. Perry

This is a work of fiction. The characters, incidents, and dialogues are
products of the author's imagination and are not to be construed as
real. Any resemblance to actual events or persons, living or dead, is
entirely coincidental.

PLAYLIST

Before I Lose My Mind (Stripped)- Ethan
Slow Dance- AJ Mitchell, Ava Max
Too Good To Be True- Rhys
Maybe It Was Me- Sody
Bury Me Deep Inside Your Heart- HIM
I Hate You, I Love You- gnash, Olivia O'Brian
Stone Cold- Demi Lovato
Call Out My Name- The Weekend
Jealous (Remix_ Nick Jonas
That's Us- Anson Seabra
I Can't Carry This Anymore- Anson Seabra
The Broken Hearts Club- gnash
Treat You Better- Shawn Mendes
Opposite Of Loving Me (Stripped)- Ethan

Listen Now on Spotify

1

Rylee

"You almost broke your face," Spencer says as he rolls to a stop in front of where I sit on the hot cement, cradling the two pieces of my busted skateboard.

No way will Mom give me another advance on my allowance. I'm three weeks in the hole as it is. Dad, on the other hand...

Spencer's words click, and I scowl up at him. "I didn't almost break my face. I landed that trick perfectly."

"Uh-huh." He swings his board up and cradles it behind his sweaty neck, propping his head on it.

"Tell me, how does your tailbone feel after that failed three-shove?" As I knock the dirt off my jean shorts, I spot a nice bruise forming on my knee. I'll never admit it, but I came close to a broken nose. And now my mom is going to kill me because I'm expected to be a lady Saturday at her friend's daughter's wedding. In two days. My whole kneecap will be purple by then.

Whoops.

Notice the lack of remorse? That's because any positive emotions I had faded away years ago.

Maybe this will be the final straw that gets me out of these ridiculous events. Church—until everyone got busy, and it fell by the wayside—weddings, family reunions. They're always so stressful. Trips to the salon. Dresses.

Makeup. My mom spends days, sometimes a week, "glamming" me up into the girl she prayed for.

Poor Mom. Tried four times for a girl and ended up with me. Not her idea of a princess. Dad doesn't seem to mind. Or, I should say, he didn't mind. I was just another one of his boys until I got my period. After that, it was all lectures about not dating and an irritated snort every time Mom forced me into something pink.

It's the reason I'll be able to guilt him into an allowance advance. If he had to choose between me being at the skate park with Spencer or me being on a date, he would choose the skate park. Without question. Every time.

The alarm on my phone goes off, making me jump. "Is it six already?"

"Afraid so." Spencer picks up his flannel shirt and slings it over his shoulder. "Want a ride home?"

I hold up the two pieces of my deck and roll my eyes. "No choice now."

Not that I would ever turn down a ride even if it's right up the road. And Spencer would never miss an opportunity to offer one. He has driven every day since he got a car for his sixteenth birthday. I would too, but being the youngest of four kids by mere minutes, I get shafted on those kinds of things.

"Might have to hose you off first," Spencer says, as he pinches his nose and leans away fanning the air.

"Please, I smell like freaking roses and rainbows." Water hits him square in the face as I cackle, wriggling away from his grabbing hand while taking a swig from my water bottle.

"Oh, you're so going to regret that!" Spencer lunges

forward, his board hitting the ground so he has both hands, and this time I don't get away.

A high-pitched squeal escapes me as he swings me up onto his shoulder, pinning my kicking legs against his chest. I struggle to breathe as he stomps through the chain-link fence drawing the attention of a group of kids sitting at a bench. My fingers dig into his lower back, allowing me enough wiggle room to lift my stomach off his shoulder and take a deep breath.

I hate that he's taller than me now.

Before I can take in our new surroundings, I'm being lifted and planted on my feet only to have my head shoved forward.

Icy water pelts my face. I press against the cold metal of what I assume is the drinking fountain, but Spencer's grip is too strong.

"Say sorry," he taunts from behind me.

"Never," I gasp once he lets go of the button. Wrong answer, because water once again blocks out my vision. I would be angrier if it weren't so refreshing. After all, we did spend all afternoon skating in the hot California sun.

After a few more seconds of waterboarding, Spencer lets me go and dances out of reach knowing I'll go right for him. I throw what he calls my death glare over my shoulder and use the hem of my shirt to wipe water droplets from my eyes.

"That's no way to treat a lady."

"Good thing there are no ladies around."

That's Spencer's and my relationship in a nutshell. We're closer than I am to my brothers. He doesn't see me as a girl about as much as I don't see him as a boy. I mean, clearly, he's a boy. But he's Spencer. Where other girls started drooling over him about the time he hit his second growth spurt and filled out, I just saw him as my best friend. And if I were ever seen as something other than one of the guys, it would be by someone other than Spencer. He's got his Rylee blinders on tight.

"What's Mom making for dinner tonight?" Spencer asks as we make our way back to our abandoned boards.

"Don't you have a family?"

"Yeah, but my mom burns water."

I pick up my busted deck and backpack. "Explain how that works again?"

"You'd have to ask her. All I know is Dad keeps four fire extinguishers around the kitchen."

"Sad."

"Very." Spencer slings a sweaty arm over my shoulder as we walk to the parking lot. "Which is why I'm so glad your mom cooks for an army every night."

"No clue what she'll do when Will goes off to college next year, and she's left with just Ryan and me."

"Continue to provide me with breakfast, lunch, and dinner?"

I shove him off me and round to the passenger side of his Toyota Camry. "Who says I'm going to keep you around that long? Junior year is coming to a close in a couple of months and summer can change a lot of things."

His hand slaps over his heart. "That hurts."

I wink as I climb inside, tossing my bag into the back seat. Spencer hops in a few seconds later and flings his sweat-covered shirt at me.

"You're disgusting." I ball up the shirt and throw it with the rest of our stuff.

Spencer smiles and starts the car. Silence is washed away by blaring music. As of late, he's been into '90s grunge. He found an old CD in his dad's office and that's what I've been subjected to since then.

I reach for the volume, but he knocks my hand away. "Driver's choice," he screams over the wailing of a guitar.

Okay. It's not as bad as I pretend it is. Some of it is great. But admitting Spencer is right about, well, anything, is a terrible idea. Someone has to keep him in his place. His head is big enough as is.

Spencer flies out of the parking lot and into traffic, coming close to a truck and making me reach for the handle above the door.

If we both hadn't taken our driving test on the same day, I would question the legitimacy of his license. Every ride comes with at least one heart-stopping moment.

A few minutes later he turns into our subdivision and switches off the music. Our neighbor Mrs. Ronald once told him she could hear his music inside her house and ever since he's taken extra effort not to disturb her because she's terrifying when angry.

Ever see a Chihuahua going after someone's ankles? Yeah, like that except instead of biting she won't hesitate to whack you upside the head with a rolled-up magazine.

Spencer pulls into his driveway and I notice right away that both of his parents' cars are missing.

"Where are the 'rents?"

He shrugs and reaches for his board and bag, but I catch the slight drop in his usual happy expression.

He's been over at my house a lot more. Not that him being around is abnormal behavior. We grew up across the street from each other and have been friends since I ran him over with my BMX bike when I was seven. But lately, it seems as if he never wants to go home.

I let the subject drop. When he's ready to talk, I'll be waiting. "Dinner in ten." I hop out and sling my backpack onto my shoulder. "Make sure to shower this time. Don't want to sit downwind from you again and lose my appetite."

"Ditto."

Jogging across the street, I wave to Mr. Clark in as he mows his impeccable yard. Seriously, it puts ours to shame, but that's because Dad put Will in charge of it and the boy is never home.

"Hey, Ma," I call as I dump my stuff by the door. The smell of lasagna hits me full force, making me salivate as my stomach rumbles in agreement.

"Hey, peanut." Her blond head comes into view, the smile dropping from her face when she takes in my soaked clothes and matted hair. "What happened?"

"What do you mean?" ask, brushing by her, grabbing a grape from the fruit bowl on the way to the fridge.

"Did you go swimming?"

"It's a billion degrees out. I dumped some water on my head."

She makes an unhappy noise, something between a sigh and a growl. "And what did you do to your elbow? Didn't I ask you to be careful?"

I twist so I can see my elbow and sure enough it's scraped and smeared with dried blood. Guess I hit more than my knee in the fall.

"It looks worse than it is." I snag a water bottle from the fridge. In two gulps I polish it off.

"That's kind of the point, Rylee. In two days you have

to wear a dress and stand in pictures and now you're covered in scratches and bruises."

"Why will I be in pictures again? I don't even know this chick. The only reason I'm going is because you're dragging me there."

Mom slams a spatula down on the counter. "Rylee Noel Everett!" I cringe at the full name drop. "I don't know what's gotten into you, but the attitude needs to stop. You throw a tantrum every single time we have a family event."

"Maybe because you parade me around like an award-winning poodle," I mutter.

Her eyebrow shoots up and I swear if looks could kill, I would not just drop dead but combust. "What was that?"

"I said I'm going to take a shower." I plant a kiss on her cheek as I walk by. There's no point in arguing with her. "Spence will be here in like five for dinner."

She nods and goes back to the stove, but I can see the tense set in her shoulders. I'll hear about this again later but from Dad.

Ryan, my twin, according to genetics, is coming down the stairs as I head up. His face is pointed down with zero attention dedicated to his surroundings. He's always glued to his phone. It's aggravating.

As I pass him, I smack the phone, making him gasp and fumble to catch it before it falls and cracks yet another screen.

"Jerk!" He snatches the back of my shirt as I try to run away. Guess I didn't think this whole thing out.

"Let go!" I tug and hear the fabric rip.

Oh, so dead.

I grab a fistful of his overgrown hair, dragging him up the last few steps so we don't tumble down. The second my foot hits the landing, he gives me a shove, forcing me to let go or slam into the wall.

"I don't want another ER visit!" My mom yells from the kitchen.

"Enough, guys." Dad steps out of their room and tears us apart, keeping us both at arm's length.

He's perfected that move over the years.

"She started it." Ryan jabs a finger in my direction, to which I stick my tongue out.

"He wasn't looking where he was going."

"I don't care whose fault it is. Both of you knock it off and get ready for dinner."

Ryan brushes a hand down the front of his shirt, smoothing out the wrinkles and rolls his eyes as our dad stupidly leaves us in the hall. It's been seventeen years, it's as if he's learned nothing.

I smile and backstep toward the bathroom. "Keep rolling your eyes. You might find your brain back there."

He lunges for me again, but I manage to slip inside the bathroom and slam the door, locking it right as the handle jiggles.

My smile widens as I hear Dad call Ryan downstairs, his tone clearly irritated.

Now I can shower in peace.

2

Spencer

"Dinner smells amazing," I say as I walk into the kitchen through the side door.

Rylee gives me a weird look, and I know it's because she beat me to the table. Out of all of us, including her brothers, I'm the only one who knows what being on time means.

I would have been on time if my mom hadn't shown up right as I was leaving. She wanted to talk, then spent fifteen minutes bitching about my dad.

Fun times.

"Didn't think you were going to make it tonight," Mrs. Everett says as she hands me a can of Coke.

I smile, but judging from the deep-set frown Rylee has going on, she senses something is wrong. Heck, she sensed it earlier in the driveway.

As my best friend, I should tell her, but she'll go into fix mode, and she can't fix my parents' marriage.

They can't even fix it.

"Dig in," Mrs. Everett says, setting the giant pan of lasagna down in the center of the table next to a bowl of garlic bread.

Mr. Everett goes about dishing it, keeping the peace because he's seen what happens if we serve ourselves. A fight always breaks out usually between Rylee and Ryan.

Rylee sits across from me next to her older brother,

Will. She has me locked in her sights and I see those wheels turning. It's been hell hiding this from her since my parents announced their separation two weeks ago. Luckily that was during spring break when Rylee and her family were off camping at the beach. By the time they got back, I'd figured out a way to mask my feelings.

"So, Spencer, how is school going?" Mrs. Everett asks as she pours a glass of wine.

"Ready for summer."

"I can't believe you guys are going to be seniors. And my Will is going to be graduating and leaving me to run off to Oregon State."

Mr. Everett shakes his head. I'm sure he's been hearing about this since January. Having their second kid go off to college, then all three of us in a year must be stressful for her. She's always been about family and I've been lucky enough to be a part of it for so long.

Little do they know that my time here might be up sooner than a year. According to my parents' whisper-yelled conversation, there's no guarantee who I will end up with or what they will do with the house.

Everyone quiets down as they shovel food in. They all act as if there won't be enough for seconds if they don't finish first. Trust me, Mrs. Everett makes enough to feed a football team. She has to with the way we all eat.

"So, are you Ry's date for the wedding Saturday?" Will asks. Rylee growls and elbows him, but he just laughs.

"Um. I hadn't planned on—"

"You should come!" Mrs. Everett claps her hands together, eyes going all puppy-dog, like every other time one of Rylee's brothers mention us dating.

It was awkward when we were eleven. It's far more

awkward now, but that's because it's hard to miss how gorgeous Rylee has gotten over the years. Standing with her brothers and making sure that no guy asks her out has gotten harder and harder. Although, her brothers might murder me if they knew the reason I was warding off the guys.

"Mom—"

"No," I cut her off. "I'd love to. I still have a suit from the last time."

Rylee cradles her face in her hands, pink splotches showing through her fingers. She hates that I'm always a default date for her. I can't say I'm equally disappointed.

———

"You don't have to come," Rylee says and hands me a bowl to load into the dishwasher.

We drew straws and lost. Well, Rylee lost, but in her world, that means I lose too.

"I don't have any other plans, what with my best friend being held hostage by a pink dress."

She scoffs and flicks soapy water at me. "You jest, but it's serious. This one has lace, Spence. Lace!"

"God forbid."

"The other day Mom straight-up told me I'll never get a boyfriend if I keep acting like one of the guys." She wipes her hands on a dishtowel and turns toward me. "First of all, I had a boyfriend freshman year—"

"That lasted a week, right?" I close the door to the dishwasher, moving to lean on the counter next to her.

"He was a Browns fan. That's unacceptable. But whatever. It's already proven her wrong. He appreciated my love of sports and that I could crush him in any video game setting."

"Must have been nice to beat someone for a change."

She pushes off the counter, snapping me with the dishtowel. "For your information, Ryan has never beaten me. And I'm pretty sure I whooped your butt hard last week in Fortnite."

True, but I'll never admit it. "What was the point of this tale again?"

"Right." She slashes her hand through the air and grabs an empty can of soda off the counter. "My point is, a dress doesn't change who I am. Deep down I'll still know all the stats of this year's draft and have my roster planned out weeks in advance for fantasy football."

"Though planning didn't save you from being crushed this year." I wince as she punches my shoulder. Growing up with three brothers, the girl knows how to hit with the perfect amount of force.

"And prancing around in pink won't win me the guy, right? Isn't it better to just be me and let the right guy find me?"

My stomach does a somersault souring the taste of the lasagna. Truth is, I've been waiting two years for her to realize I'm her perfect match, but it seems I'm so deep in the friend zone I'm not even a blip on her radar.

"Jax, for example," she carries on not noticing the pained expression on my face when she drops his name. The guy is a tool not worthy of thinking about Ry. "He said I had mad basketball skills when he saw me in PE. Scrubbed out and sweaty as all hell. Tell me that's not a great foundation for a relationship."

"Jax dates cheerleaders. Girls who don't know the first

thing about sports besides how to shake a pom-pom and do the splits."

"That's not true. I actually had a conversation with Hannah and she matched my level of knowledge when it comes to football. You're just bitter because Haylee turned you down for homecoming."

"To go out with Jax."

Her lower lip juts out in the most adorable pout. "So, you're agreeing with my mom. To get a guy, I need to change who I am."

"No." I gather the rest of the garbage off the counter and throw it into the bin with a bit too much force. "What I'm saying is that you need to find the right guy. One who appreciates you for you."

"But the only guy who does is you."

Exactly! I scream inside my head.

"And even you date the exact same girl you just described for Jax. So am I going to be alone forever doomed to live with ten cats who eventually eat me when I die and no one notices all because I got stuck with three brothers and a dad who had a football jersey picked out for me before the doctor delivered the blow that I was a girl?" She takes a deep breath after her epic one-breath rant.

I place my hands on her shoulders and give them a shake. "What I think is that you should focus on getting through this wedding. Then we can go through the year-book one page at a time so I can tell you why each guy at our school isn't worthy of your attention. Especially Jax."

Rylee's face lights up with a smile as I pull her in for a hug.

I'm going to miss this.

"I gotta get home. Need my beauty sleep." I throw a wink over my shoulder as I slip out the side door.

My dad's car is still gone. He's been staying at the local Holiday Inn. No clue what they're going for, but our neighbors are bound to notice his absence pretty soon. They can keep the separation quiet for only so long. And when it blows up, I'll have to tell Rylee that our plan of ruling Roseville High senior year then running off to Oregon State is about as likely as the Browns winning the Super Bowl.

Or as likely as her realizing I'm the guy she's been wishing for.

3

Rylee

"How'd you do on the pop quiz?" I ask Spencer as we make our way down the jam-packed hallway. It's Friday, and everyone is so ready to get out of here.

"Crashed and burned. Mrs. Miller said she'll be offering extra credit next week. I'll need it so I don't have to retake World History."

"And pass eleventh grade." I sidestep a group of kids loitering by the exit. "I'd hate to leave you behind when I run off to Oregon."

Spencer flashes me a tight smile and rubs the back of his neck. As of late, that's his reaction every single time I bring up college. If he has other plans, he'd better tell me soon because I'm banking on him being there with me as freshmen.

"So. Wedding tomorrow." Spencer twists his baseball hat around and squints at me. "What level of stress monster will your mom be?"

"Twelve."

"The scale only goes to ten."

"Exactly." I drop my new board on the ground and place a foot on it. "You know how she is with these kinds of things. Always the perfect family. One of these times I swear I'm going to roll up in some ripped jeans and let loose an F-bomb. Watch her face melt right off."

"No, you won't. Not until you're about to move out, that is."

"Truth-bomb and run? Sure to make holidays awkward for the foreseeable future."

I push off with my right foot, rolling down the crowded sidewalk, zigzagging in and out of people as Spencer follows behind. We will ultimately end up at the skate park, but we hate waiting in traffic to get out of school. Plus, riding around on campus usually pisses off a few teachers, which is a happy bonus.

Hey, they piss us off daily with their pop quizzes and group projects where only one person does the bulk of the work. We have to take our shots where we can.

"Movie night tonight?" Spencer asks from behind me.

I swivel my head his way then crash into something, feeling the impact in my stomach before losing my footing. Air leaves my body as I tumble to the ground, catching my forearm on the cement first and sending a jolt through the rest of my arm. A faint groan follows the collision alerting me to the fact that it was someone I ran into and not something.

With a palm on my throbbing forehead, I sit up and first see Spencer jogging toward me, with concern written all over his face. The fall was brutal so I'm sure it looks nasty. And if it's nasty for me, I can only imagine what the poor bystander feels.

"I'm so sor—" My gaze lands on a face that has made a nightly appearance in my dreams the past few months. All words leave me as gorgeous blue eyes stare back at me...with a large dose of irritation.

"Jax," I sigh, as I dust the dirt off the knees of my jeans

hoping he didn't hear the longing in my voice. "I'm so sorry. I didn't see you there."

"Looking helps with that." Jax pushes up, the muscles in his forearms flexing from the effort, and offers me a hand. "You okay?"

The second my skin touches his rainbows shoot across the sky. Unicorns fart glitter. Fireworks erupt in every single one of my nerves...and I lose the ability to think straight.

"Uh, yeah. Great," I stammer, trying and failing to regain my composure. "Well, not great. Kinda feels like I ran into a wall. Which, hey, good for you." I land a soft punch to his arm then cringe, realizing I might give myself away.

Stop talking.

Spencer returns to my side, holding my board. It must have flown off somewhere in the crash. Thank goodness he found it before a car crushed it because I'm pretty sure I won't be able to convince my dad to sneak me another advance to replace it.

"So..." Jax pivots toward the school, his eyes ticking between Spencer and me and I swear he looks as if I might give him cooties or run him over again. "See you later?" He doesn't wait for any kind of response before walking away toward a group of guys laughing their asses off.

I let my head drop into my cupped hands. "I'm such an idiot."

"Not an idiot. Just...awkward."

I glare at him through my splayed fingers. "*So* much better."

Spencer hands over my board and shrugs. "Why do you care?"

"Uh, hello. I mowed over the guy I'm in love with." The last part comes out as a whisper. I know Jax can't hear me since he's rounded the corner and I've lost sight of him, but still. Can't be too safe.

Spencer's nose wrinkles. "In love? Come on. You've said a total of thirty words to the guy. How are you in love?"

"Shut up!" I shove him, my whole face burning because, Jesus, he kinda screamed the whole 'me loving Jax' thing. "Keep your voice down."

"Okay." Spencer holds his hands up and laughs. "But seriously. Crushes aren't the same as love. You gotta know someone way better than that to love them."

"Says Mr. Two Semi-Serious Girlfriends?"

"That's a long pet name." Spencer nudges me and walks off toward the parking lot.

I jog after him, grimacing at the pain in my knee. Walking in heels tomorrow should be fun.

"Just admit that you have no clue what being in love feels like." I catch up to him and fall in line with his wide strides. *Glad I got my father's height.* "You've dated two girls all through high school and have gone out with a handful of other girls once."

"Which gives me more experience to say you can't fall in love with someone you don't know."

"Jax hangs out with Will all the time."

Spencer unlocks his car with a sigh. "And you hide in your room or over at my house. Again, having a crush doesn't equal love."

"I don't hide." He throws me a *yeah sure,* look. "Okay,

fine." I toss my bag and board into his back seat. "But that's only because my mouth freaks out every single time he's around. I either go mute or can't stop words from flying out and smacking his eardrums with my stupidity."

Spencer's boisterous laugh fills the cab of the car as he pulls out of the parking spot and turns toward the road. "If only you could find a guy you are comfortable talking to without going into spaz mode."

"Never going to happen. The only people who fall into that category are my brothers—gross—and you." My phone dings in my pocket and I reach to grab it, not quite catching whatever grumbly thing Spencer mumbles.

I groan and bang my head on the seat when I see my mom's text. "No skate park today. Mom says I already have enough bumps and bruises."

"Well...there goes our afternoon." Spencer taps his chin as we pull up to a red light. "Movie night?"

"Only if we stop at Edwin's first for an Oreo shake."

"Think your mom will approve since you have to fit into a dress tomorrow?"

The devious smile Spencer throws my way makes his brown eyes sparkle. Geez, if I notice it, no wonder girls are always throwing themselves at him. These past few years, he's transformed from a gangly kid into well, hot. Okay, yes, I think my best friend is hot. I would have to be blind *not* to see it. But where his smile melts the rest of the female population into a pile of goop, it just bounces right off my Spencer-shield. The shield that popped up the day he ate a worm from my backyard. And, okay, I did dare him, but still.

That was the day he cemented his title as best friend. Even if I felt differently, there's nothing in the world that would make me risk that. Not even his perfect smile that became braces free last year but never lost the mischief. Or the way he makes me feel safe with every hug.

Spencer is my constant and I'll never compromise what we have.

———

"Why are we watching this again?" Spencer whines as he fluffs my pillows and leans against the wooden headboard my dad made last year.

"Because it's my favorite." I tuck my legs underneath me as I scroll through our available titles, searching for tonight's entertainment.

"How are you not sick of watching it?"

"Beautiful cars. Paul Walker. There will never be another combo quite like that." I press Play when I reach *The Fast and the Furious* and fall back on my now pillowless bed. "Think I can have one of those?" I tug on the corner of my black pillowcase, but Spencer doesn't budge.

"No way. If I have to suffer through this again, then you can be just as uncomfortable as me." He sighs and stretches, bringing his hands to rest behind his head.

"Spencer." As I lean forward he smirks. No fear anymore. It used to be so much easier beating him up when I weighed more than him.

"I'll trade you. A pillow for a new movie."

The opening scene plays behind me but I've focused solely on my bed-hogging best friend. "You're bargaining *my* pillows in *my* bedroom? I could just kick you out."

He pinches my chin between his thumb and forefinger. "But you would never do that."

A car revs and I really want to turn my attention to Paul Walker, but Mr. Smug needs to be dealt with. "And if I ask you to leave and never come back?" I lean forward until our noses are touching.

Spencer sucks in a sharp breath. "Then you would spend your nights with your mom. Face it, Everett, you need me here as a buffer. Besides, how boring would your life be without me?"

"I'd say it would be an improvement." I reach for my pillow again, but Spencer is faster and snags my wrist. "Bad move, Hendricks." With a hand behind his head and the other holding my wrist, he leaves himself open for the one thing he's never grown out of.

My fingertips dig into his ribs and he immediately convulses under me, almost bucking me off the bed. His free hand shoves into my shoulder, but I lean into it doubling my efforts until he's laughing so hard his eyes are watering.

"Give me a pillow!"

"Nev...er..." he gasps and rolls to the side, crumpling in a ball and cutting off my access to his ribs. He's breathing heavily and the look he throws over his shoulder screams of revenge.

I yelp and try to roll away, but he's way faster. Before I know what's happening, I'm pinned under his full weight and he's going for the one spot on my body where I'm ticklish. The one place I can't protect. My stupid knee.

I mean, who is ticklish on the knee?

Tears spring to my eyes as I fight the laughter and him. This is the exact reason I miss being taller and bigger than him. When he was a runt, I could take him down no problem.

We must have been louder than I thought because my door bangs open and Will's annoyed face comes into view.

"Didn't Mom say no boys in your bedroom? Oh wait, it's just Spencer." Will leans against the doorframe and grins. "Do you both wear date repellant or something? It's Friday night—why are you home?"

"You're home." I shove Spencer off me and sit up. "But I'd wager a guess it's just your face that's a repellant."

Spencer laughs but covers it up with a cough. For some reason, he's always been a little scared of Will.

"For your information, Mom made me cancel a date because she wants me rested for the wedding. I'm guessing you're home because no one wants to spend time around you. Especially when you're together."

Spencer drops his gaze to the bed and my cheeks heat with anger. Before I can come up with a comeback Will is shutting the door.

"You might as well date each other. No one else will want you," Will calls as the door clicks shut.

"Ass," I mumble and smooth out my hair. "He's just grumpy because Ellie dumped him last week.

Spencer nods and glances at the clock above my TV. "I should get home—it's pretty late."

"It's nine."

He stands and ruffles my hair. "Yeah, but much like Will, I need my beauty rest."

"Try to look better than me tomorrow."

"Impossible." His eyes find mine for a second before he sighs. "See ya tomorrow."

After he leaves, I grab all the pillows that went flying during the war of the bed and pile them up. I try to concentrate on the movie, but Will's voice keeps wiggling its way into my thoughts. Nothing would be better than making him eat his own words. Maybe it's time I tried the whole dating thing again.

4

Rylee

"Laugh and you die."

Spencer stands by the front door looking amazing as always in his dark blue suit and black tie. To my surprise, his hair is slicked back giving me an unobstructed view of his face, which at the moment is trying to remain passive.

I adjust the evil contraption that is a push-up bra for the thousandth time since putting it on. Whoever invented underwire should be hung. With underwire.

I clutch the matching blush-colored heels my mom bought yesterday as I trudge down the rest of the steps. Didn't trust myself not to get caught on the carpet and swan dive onto the hardwood floor.

Although a hospital visit is a far better alternative than another stupid wedding.

To my dismay, Spencer can no longer hide the amusement on his face when I stop at the base of the stairs. His lips are pinned between his teeth and I swear he's seconds from suffocating on his own laugh.

"Tell me I'm beautiful." I sink down on the bottom step and slide my right foot into the shoe of death Mom calls slingbacks.

"Only you could pull off that shade of pink," Spence says, extending a hand once my shoes are on, knowing I could break an ankle if I got up on my own.

"Hideous, right?" I smooth out the front, then adjust

the satin bow at my waist. I would never admit it out loud, but the dress isn't as hideous on as I'd thought it would be. It gives me curves I never knew I had and my mom was smart enough to buy something with quarter sleeves and a longer hemline to cover my inevitable bruises.

Tell me again why she made a big deal about the scratch on my elbow?

"It looks great even though I can tell you're itching to throw on a pair of Chucks." He tucks one of the curls my mom spent way too long creating behind my ear, making me smile. If she knew someone was messing with her work, her head would explode.

"You have no idea," I whisper.

"No idea about what?" My dad asks as he walks out of the kitchen, buttoning up his suit jacket.

"How hard it is to walk in heels." I beam at him and watch his facial expression sour as he's once again reminded he has a daughter and not four boys.

"Doesn't she look lovely?" Mom asks as she follows him out. Her eyes are glistening.

If she cries, I bail.

She manages to keep her emotions in check and turns to Spencer. "Aren't you handsome? You two always look so great together," she says and flattens out a wayward strand of hair at the nape of Spencer's neck.

I have to admit, he did a good job reining in his wild locks.

"Thank you, Mrs. Everett." His face scrunches as she gives him a quick peck on the cheek leaving behind a bright red smear.

I point to my cheek, letting him know to clean it off

before turning toward the stairs. "Idiot one and idiot two, we're ready!"

"Rylee, language," Mom admonishes.

I shrug. "Not bad language if it's true." Dad tries to hide his smile behind a fist and Spencer shakes his head, opening the door in a not-so-subtle maneuver to separate himself from me before drawing Mom's ire.

Spencer and I walk toward the driveway as Mom waits behind for Will and Ryan. It's a family event, which means she needs to assess everyone's wardrobe and make sure that their suits match well with Dad's.

After all, what would happen if all of them were in clashing colors?

Pretty sure the world would end.

"So how long did this take?" Spencer grabs my hand and twirls me, causing me to dole out one of my rare squeals when I'm caught off guard.

"Hours. So many painful hours." He tugs me to his chest and I let my hands rest on his shoulders. With heels I'm eye-level and he can't hide the ever-present mischievous glint. "You gonna save me a dance later or will you be too busy with the sad single chicks Will is always going on about?"

"The only sad single chick I want to spend time with is you." He boops me on the nose and I resist the urge to punch him.

According to my mom, I can't go a single day without laying into someone. I took that bet and now my allowance advance is riding on it. Well, advance times two, because I forgot to mention Dad already gave me money for a new board. *Oops.*

Spencer takes a step backward as the rest of my

family joins us. Will smirks and elbows Ryan who is too absorbed in his phone to notice the somewhat intimate embrace Spencer and I were in.

You would think they would be used to it by now. We don't see each other that way so why would a lingering hug matter?

Dad shoos us toward his Yukon, taking the lead before Mom has a brain aneurysm. Being on time means we're late in her eyes. To make the best impression we need to be there close to an hour early. It gives her the most time to show off her *perfect* family.

Insert eye roll.

If her friends saw us all in a normal setting, they might think we've been body-snatched.

———

Twenty minutes later thanks to traffic on Douglas Boulevard, which dragged out the painfully silent ride, we pull into the parking lot of the Sierra Vista Country Club. It's got money and class written all over it and now I'm all too aware of why Mom's been fidgeting the whole drive.

I heard her mention something about her friend's daughter marrying into money, but I guess it didn't click as anything important until now.

We all unload from the car and as we pass, she makes sure to do a final once-over, straightening Will's tie and snatching Ryan's phone. She'll keep it in her purse for the rest of the day, which will surely put him into a foul mood.

As Spencer and I pass, Mom untucks the strand of hair Spencer pushed behind my ear earlier, letting out a huff and mumbling about ruining the overall shape of the curl.

I widen my eyes at Spencer over Mom's shoulder. The only bonus to heels is that I'm taller than she is. He pretends not to see me, focusing on straightening his tie before my mom can get to him.

Suck-up.

My mom gives Spencer a warm smile and a pat on the back as she passes and he extends his arm to me, readying himself to be my escort for the night. Poor sap. I don't know why he caved so easily. I would have given my left arm to get out of this.

"You think they're going to check our bank accounts at the door?" he whispers.

Ah. He caught it too. As if I didn't feel out of place already. Now we'll have to be on extra good behavior. Total fun suck. Like visiting Grandma.

"I hope so. Save us from having to sit through this."

"Bet the food will be good though."

"Oh, bonkers good. You have a strong argument there. This torture might be worth the food. Ugh...and think about the cake. Bet it's at least five tiers and has pearls."

"No way. Four tiers with those edible flowers that taste like old marshmallows."

It's clear we've been roped into too many weddings together.

"You're on." I extend my free hand.

"Loser gets to pick the next movie and all the snacks." He grabs my hand before I can object. He knows I hate relinquishing movie power.

Mom throws a dirty look over her shoulder as I laugh a little too loud and give Spencer a shove when he refuses to let go of my fingers. The smile drops from my face and I throw my shoulders back, putting on the perfect daughter facade I've perfected after all these years.

We're led around a building and toward rows and rows of white chairs all adorned with blush pink bows and flowers.

Did my mom match me to the freaking decor?

This is a new low. Even for her.

My tight smile twitches, settling into what I assume resembles a grimace. Spencer's hand wrapping around mine and giving it a squeeze is the only thing that stops me from going guestzilla right here in the middle of the rose-covered walkway.

The usher leads us to our seats. Right up front. No surprise there. I position myself at the end as far away from my mother as possible. If I plan on keeping it together through this whole god-awful event—and I do for future sanity sake—I need distance.

Spencer doesn't release my hand even once we've relaxed into our chairs. Not that I mind much. Sucking up all his positive energy will keep me on track. He has the superhuman ability to read my emotions and stop me before saying or doing something I'll regret. He's the C-3PO to my R2-D2. The Silent Bob to my Jay. He's rational when I can't keep my thoughts—let alone my emotions—in check. And out of everyone, he's very aware of what my mother does to me.

I dab my glistening forehead with a tissue I had the forethought to store in my bra. Whoever thought an outside wedding was a good idea in Northern California must have been out of their mind. Even in the shade, the sun tortures. It's barely spring, but the heat has already swooped in. Though I guess I should be happy it's not a June wedding. We would all have heatstroke by the time the ceremony was over.

Thirty tortuous minutes later the processional starts. Couples file down the aisle to a freaking string quartet. Haven't they heard of sound systems? Boom. Press of a button and any song ever recorded can be played instantaneously. No need to go all-out and have live music. Not unless it's a concert of course.

I'm about to lean over and tell Spencer we should up the ante because they definitely will have pearls on the cake if they are going this traditional when one of the groomsmen catches my eye. Hello, I would know those broad shoulders and scrumptious jaw anywhere. Jaxxon Lever passes right by me—so close I could reach out and touch him if I wanted— with a gorgeous blonde on his arm.

My grip must have tightened in response to my increased heart rate because Spencer's head swivels my direction, eyebrows scrunched in. It only takes him a second to catch on and follow my gaze to where Jax now stands next to a man who bears a striking resemblance. Oh, holy hell. The groom is Jax's brother. I'd seen him in a couple of photos shared on Instagram.

Yes. I might have cyberstalked Jax a little bit. But only when bored because he is always doing something fun. Beach trips. Boating. Snowboarding. Never a dull moment on his page. And the fact that he is drool-worthy might be, okay, totally, is the main drawing factor.

I've had a crush on him since freshman year when I slammed into him and nearly broke my neck. It was Spencer's fault of course. He had challenged me to a race down the school halls with a whole month's allowance on the line.

I'll never forget the look of shock moments before colliding that transformed into what resembled disgust. Hey, in my defense I was a freshman and still thought it was cool to wear my older brother's shirts that swamped my body. And I might have been going through a pixie cut phase that I upped the ante on by dying bright pink—much to Mom's dismay.

Obvious disdain aside, it didn't stop fireworks from lighting my chest or the slowing of time as I stared into the most gorgeous blue eyes I had ever seen. My crush only rolled further out of control over the years as he got taller and filled out in all the yummiest places.

This is all too much. Fate is trying to tell me Jax is my soulmate. Why else would we literally run into each other twice in two years? And now he's here.

Freaking Mom. She didn't tell me her friend's daughter was marrying Zack Lever. That's a huge detail to leave out. Their father is one of the most affluential real estate agents in the area. They live in Granite Bay in a ginormous mansion. Even though they have money coming out the ears, they never seem to flaunt it. Jax goes to Roseville High, which must be a step down from Granite Bay. Looking at the wedding with new eyes it seems as if they pulled back a lot.

No wonder Mom was on edge. Now I am too.

Jax is here. We've never spent one moment outside of school together seeing as we don't run in the same circles. The only thing we have in common is Will and they have more of a passing friendship. But he's here now. And I'm here. My eyes drop to my lap. And I'm wearing a pink dress.

Thanks again, Mom.

The bride walks down the aisle. Things are said. Some sand is poured into a jar. Spencer's hand holds on to mine, but all I can focus on is Jax's face and the sweat that must be pooling under my armpits.

Once the ceremony ends and everyone has filed down the aisle, I jump up, dragging Spencer with me. There are drapey tents set up not far off and I can guarantee there is air-conditioning. I don't want to look like a sweaty pig when I run into Jax. Fingers crossed it's not a physical run-in this time.

We're five steps away when my father's booming voice stops me dead in my tracks.

"Rylee. Pictures. She'll meet you in there, Spencer."

Spencer cringes as he steps back. "I'll snag you some appetizers. You know they'll have mini potpies or something."

I leave Spencer with the other guests and trek down to where I can see the wedding party taking photos. Mom is standing close to her friend Sophia, with an arm around Will and even from several feet away I can tell she's gushing. When her eyes find me, her face lights up and she waves me over.

"Sophia, you remember Rylee." I smile and wiggle my fingers, sliding into the spot that Will vacated in a rush. Lucky jerk. "She's a year below Zack's brother."

"Oh, yes. I'm sure Jaxxon will be happy to have more people his age. I can't imagine weddings are much fun for teenagers."

A breathy giggle escapes me and soon after heat

rushes to my cheeks. Jax may be happy there are other people his age here, but he won't be happy to see me. What will probably happen is he'll spot Will and they'll be stuck together all night. Not that I would have the guts to approach him. Secret crushes are meant to stay secret. And when I get nervous, I have a hard time controlling my mouth.

Mom and Sophia go about talking as if I'm not there. That doesn't mean Mom releases me from my perfect daughter routine. Nope. I'm stuck to her side through one of the most boring conversations known to man and then the gazillion photos I'm forced to smile for. The only upside is the few I got to take with the whole wedding party. Even though the evil photographer placed Jax all the way on the other side where he couldn't see me.

Who has random guests take photos with the bride and groom, anyway?

Okay, yes, my mom has been friends with Sophia for years, but I've said maybe ten words to her daughter. For crying out loud, I don't even know her name.

Maggie. Or Molly. It's definitely an *M* name. Not that it matters much, I'm just trying to get through the rest of the night without embarrassing myself. Tall order for me.

———

"Did you hear me?" Spencer asks from the chair next to me.

The reception has been in full swing for at least an hour and yet, my tummy hasn't seen any of the awesome food I was promised. Not even a mini potpie.

"No. Sorry." I pull a funny face that gets Spencer to laugh and wipes the annoyed look away.

"I said, Ryan was mentioning sneaking away to go hit some balls on the course. Wanna join?"

I motion to my dress, then sneak a peek at my mom. She may have let me out of her sight but she'd kill me if I messed up her dress. Notice how I didn't say my dress? Yeah, it will retire to her closet with all the other clothes I've worn once.

"As fun as that sounds, I'll be dead if I got a single speck of dirt on this lacy monstrosity. Besides, I need food before I go all Godzilla on this joint."

He holds his hand up. "I swear, there wasn't a single passed appetizer. I'm as shocked as you."

"What he means is that we ate them all." Ryan leans into our conversation and smirks. "You don't like sliders anyway, right?"

I clench my fists and want so badly to sock him in the arm. As if sensing it, Dad looks over and shakes his head.

Stupid parental ESP.

I settle for sticking out my tongue, which is rewarded with laughter from both Spencer and Ryan. You would think Spencer was Ryan's best friend with the way they've been acting tonight.

"How about you two go frolic and play and I'll save your dinner for you when it comes."

"What you mean is you'll eat it out of spite," Spencer mumbles into his glass of water.

"Exactly."

Alas, my plan never comes to pass because as soon as the word is out of my mouth, the waiters start bringing out plates of food.

I can't tell what it is, but at this point, I would eat anything including tofu.

A few minutes later a glorious steak is set down in front of Spencer. My stomach rumbles with joy that turns into an acid shower when a salad is set in front of me.

Not even a good salad either with crispy chicken and cheese and glazed nuts. This is some vegan rabbit food that has far too many green things on it. My lips pull down into a frown, which causes Ryan to lean back with laughter.

I take back the tofu thing.

I poke the stupid thing with my fork, then whimper. This is my mother's doing.

"Want my steak?" Spencer nudges his plate toward me.

By this time my mom has joined us at the table and judging from the arch in her eyebrow, she knows what Spencer just said.

"No." I blow a strand of hair out of my face. "But we gotta stop by Squeeze tomorrow. I'll need some red meat to balance out whatever this is."

"Deal."

With a final sigh, I dig into the salad. I guess it's better than nothing at all.

5
Spencer

Rylee has never looked more adorable than while
scowling at the lettuce stuck to her fork. She picks the
lettuce out of her burgers for crying out loud so I'm sure
every bite is pure torture.

I try to eat my steak as subtlety as possible so I don't
rub it in her face more, but it's kind of hard when every
few seconds she glances my way with longing in her
beautiful brown eyes.

During one of those lingering glances, her mom turns
away to talk to another guest a few tables over. I take the
opportunity to cut a gigantic piece out of my steak, then
shove it toward her mouth.

She lunges forward without hesitation then leans
back moaning. It's kind of loud and gives off crazy sexual
vibes causing a few heads to turn to our way including
Ryan who simply rolls his eyes and nudges me in
the side.

"Those two smoking hot bridesmaids at the end of
the table over there said they would *love* to learn how to
handle balls."

"You're revolting." Rylee crumples her napkin and
throws it at Ryan's face.

"Hey, I'm not the one who said it. Don't shoot
the repeater."

"Not a saying."

"Sure it is."

I lean backward as they lean closer trying not to yell as they hurl insults at each other. It's a common occurrence. One I've learned how to navigate. If I break it up too soon, one or both will seek revenge in some painful and colorful fashion. If I wait too long, fists with be thrown. A delicate balance.

Rylee reaches for her water and that's my cue to step in.

"People are making their way to the dance floor. Wanna show 'em how it's done?" I extend my hand to Rylee, ignoring the overdramatic gagging sounds from Ryan.

I may have met Rylee first, but they're a package deal and over the years Ryan and I have morphed into friends much to Rylee's dismay. The thing is, it was inevitable. Growing up in that house meant I spent a lot of time with her brothers. They became my family too. Part of what kept me from ever admitting my feelings for Rylee out loud. Not only would I lose her, but I would risk losing three brothers in the process.

With one last glare thrown at Ryan, Rylee stands and takes my hand, igniting the familiar buzz in my chest when we touch. "Might as well make the most of our time here."

I couldn't agree more.

Rylee wobbles on her heels as I haul her to the edge of the wooden dance floor. Multicolored lights flash as the music picks up. I take the opportunity to whirl her around, laughing as she squeals and clings to my shoulders for support.

"Don't break my ankle!" she yells as I place her on the

ground. "It won't make you better than me on the rail even with a cast."

"How do those delusions fit in your head?"

I spin her away from me before she can answer, clutching her hand so she doesn't slam into the older couple behind her. When I yank her back, she's panting and I can tell the height of her heels is making her nervous.

"Kick off those death traps," I shout over the heavy beat of some song I've heard my mom play in her office.

Rylee nibbles on her lower lip, shooting a glance to where her mom sits watching us.

"You've already done the pictures and the meet and greet. Kick 'em off!"

She bobs her head once and reaches down to undo the straps at her ankles. Two swift kicks later, her shoes are in a pile in the corner of the dance floor and she's back to her appropriate height. Tall enough to wrap her arms around my neck, but short enough for me to prop my chin on her head. It wasn't always this way. At one point she was taller than me, and advantage she used to beat me into submission when I didn't want to play whatever crazy game she came up with that day.

"She's watching, isn't she?" Rylee asks as the song switches to a slow love ballad and I pull her flush against my chest.

Right where she should be.

"Who cares?"

"She's gotten worse about it this last year. I think for the longest time she was waiting for this *phase* to end. Like one day I would wake up and no longer love sports and skateboarding." Her voice dips enough that I have to lean down to hear her, pressing my cheek against hers. "I know I'm not the daughter she hoped for, but I'm still her kid, right?"

"You're perfect."

Rylee leans away, the flashy lights making her eyes sparkle. "You have to say that."

God, I want to kiss her. Those pouty lips of hers have become an obsession, haunting my dreams and tempting me every waking minute. If for one second I thought she felt the same way, I would have jumped into the deep end years ago. Screw what her brothers would think or the inevitable ass kicking. But she doesn't. She's made that abundantly clear with all the lusty looks she's thrown Jax's way tonight not to mention every single time she sees him in the hall.

"You okay?" she asks.

Wow. Guess I spaced out there for a second. "Yeah, of course."

"Really? Because you looked like you were seconds away from killing someone. I've only seen that look when Jace Williams took my board and tried to ride down the halls with it." She pokes the space between my eyebrows. "And that was in the sixth grade."

"And he deserved the split lip I gave him."

"Violence is never the answer."

"Says the girl who uses her fists far more often than words."

"Hey, I learned at a young age that was the only way to survive in a houseful of boys."

"You just proved my point."

"Ladies and gentlemen," the DJ announces over the

speakers. "If you would please make your way off the dance floor. It's time for the couple's first dance."

"Wanna sneak out of here?" I ask as Rylee stoops to pick up her shoes.

We both peek at her mom who is busy chatting up another guest.

"Definitely!"

I grab her hand again and we dash for the exit. Warm air smacks me in the face as we round the tent toward the back. For a brief second, I think we will have a chance to be alone, but then two forms come into view followed by obnoxious laughter.

Will leans against one of the tent's support poles as Jax stands in front of him, talking animatedly.

When we get within a few feet of them and I can hear the inappropriate story Jax is telling about one of the freshman cheerleaders, I clear my throat.

Will's eyes swing to us and narrow. "What do you want, pip-squeak?"

"I'm one year younger than you, numbnuts."

"Rylee, is that you?" Jax interrupts the siblings. "I hardly recognized you."

"That's what a pound of makeup will do," Will says, but I catch the warning tone in his voice and the way he stands up straighter.

"Says the guy who used coverup for his senior pictures." Rylee's voice breaks and her eyes shoot to Jax. "Hey, Jax."

I stand by her side, taking in the fact that neither boy has acknowledged my presence. I'm used to it with Will. Ever since he became a senior, he thinks his shit don't stink. Jax, on the other hand, can't seem to take his eyes off Rylee which is sending fire through my veins.

"You look good," he says, and a smile lights Rylee's face at Jax's words.

I told her as much earlier, but I guess my words mean nothing.

"Dude." Will shoves Jax's shoulder making him stumble. "That's my sister."

"I'm sorry. It's just...she..." Jax motions to Rylee and clears his throat. "Just used to seeing her all sweaty in gym is all. You clean up nice."

Rylee's cheeks flame red. "Oh. Well...thanks?" Her gaze flits to me, eyes wide.

I know that look. Best friend intervention time.

"Well, we should get back. I'm sure your mom is wondering where we ran off to." I nudge her with my shoulder as I turn and head back toward the front of the tent.

Rylee lopes after me, holding her heels to her chest. Once we round the front, she grabs on to my sleeve and swings me around.

"Oh my God. Jax said I looked good. And he's noticed me in gym. This is huge. Bigger than huge. What's bigger than huge?" She palms her forehead. "This is my opening. If I play it right maybe...I don't know. But this is it, Spencer! I can feel it."

"Rylee—"

"I just need to focus. Come on." She tugs me toward the entrance. "Let's get back before my mom makes a scene and crushes any chance I have."

I follow after her, feeling the weight of our relationship pressing down on me. Any chance I had at steering us out of the friend zone was just crushed like a freaking bug on the freeway.

But I guess it doesn't matter much. A few months from now I'll be a fleeting memory. Might as well let those hopes be crushed now before I end up as bitter as my father.

6

Rylee

"So." I relax into my chair and take a sip of my soda. Spencer and I spent all afternoon at the skate park and nothing in life has ever tasted as amazing.

"So," Spencer parrots and shoves half of his burger into his mouth in an impressive, yet disgusting, display.

"A thought occurred to me when those two hot chicks rolled up and pretty much every boy within a mile radius stopped what they were doing to drool and stare. Including you." I punctuate my words by throwing a fry at his face. He catches it in his mouth and grins.

"What's the point you're trying to make here?"

"My point is that maybe my mom is right."

Spencer coughs, choking on the soda he just drank. I toss him some napkins and lean back, crossing my arms.

"What did you say? I think misheard you," he asks once his lungs calm down.

"Don't make me repeat myself. Was hard enough thinking it let alone saying it out loud."

"I've just...I never thought I would see the day when you admitted your mom was right about something."

I take a bite of my burger and talk through the food. "That's because she's never been right before."

He shoots me a *yeah sure* look but doesn't say anything. Mom and I have a *unique* relationship. It's not at all what I assume most girls have, much to her dismay.

Mine too, believe me. Life would be way easier if we got along for more than five seconds a day.

"So, what was she right about?"

I steal a glance at the other patrons. There's no one around I know, but can't be too safe.

Probably should have had this conversation in the privacy of Spencer's car.

"Never mind. It's dumb." I stand with my tray and take it over to the trash. Spencer follows, dumping the wrappers that came with our meal and his pickles. The weirdo has a grudge against pickles for some reason.

"I gotta know what's going on in that head of yours." He nudges me as we walk across the parking lot to his car. "If it made you admit your mom was right about something it must be good."

"Well..." I nibble the corner of my lip, catching on a dry piece of skin. ChapStick might be in order when we're going to be outside in the heat all day.

"Out with it, Everett." Spencer unlocks the car, but stops in front of the passenger door, blocking me from getting in.

Stupid jerk knows me too well. I planned on cranking up the music so I wouldn't have to continue talking about what I now realize is the most ridiculous idea on the planet.

"What do two girls in short-shorts have to do with your mom?"

I groan and toss my head back, thankful that clouds have rolled in and blocked out the sun otherwise I might be blinded. Along with ChapStick, I need to remember to bring my sunglasses.

"We can stand here all day."

I throw him a glare, but move to his side, leaning up against the door next to him. "I was thinking that my mom might be right about the whole tomboy thing. You saw the way Jax looked at me last night and I saw the way you and every other guy looked at those girls. Junior year is essentially over and I would like to have at least one long-term boyfriend before graduating."

"Oh...kay..." Spencer's eyebrows furrow as he peers down at me.

"So maybe you could help me be...I don't know... more girly?"

Those furrowed brows shoot up widening his eyes. "How the hell am I supposed to teach you how to be more girly? Isn't this a job for your mom?"

My fingers rub circles on my temples as a headache works its way to the surface. "Do you understand how miserable she'll make life if I involve her? Besides, getting a guy's perspective will be far more helpful. You date the same type of girls as Jax and you'll be able to coach me on what not to say and how to dress." I press my fingertips together and pout my lower lip. "Please?"

The shocked expression hasn't left his face. In fact, it's morphed into a shocked-slash-appalled look I've never seen before. It's impressive.

"I'm a lost cause, huh? Forget I said anything. Was a stupid idea." I tug on the handle, popping the door open and knocking Spencer back a few steps. "Just please don't mention this to Ryan. He'll never let it go and I'd like to not spend senior year in jail for twin murder."

I hop in the car and watch as Spencer rounds to the driver's side on wooden legs. He looks kind of pale and now I feel stupid for even bringing it up. Guess people can't change. I'll always be Rylee Everett. Local tomboy and lost cause.

A few miles down the road, Spencer turns down the music and sucks in a deep breath. "So, let me get this straight. You want me to help you be like the type of girls Jax dates. Am I getting this right?"

"Paraphrased, but yeah."

"And that will make you happy? Jax will make you happy?" His voice cracks a bit on Jax's name and he quickly clears his throat.

"At the risk of sounding shallow...yes. Jax heads off to college in the fall with Will. It's my last chance to at least try. Strike while the iron is hot and I'm fresh on his mind from the wedding."

Spencer nods, tapping his thumbs on the steering wheel as we wait at a red light.

"I get that it sounds ridiculous. But what if this is my shot? What if I've missed out on a ton of crap because I refused to give an inch with my mom? Seems she might have been right all along and I was too stubborn to see it. And I'll kill you if you ever repeat any of this to my mom or brothers."

"You don't need to change yourself for a guy." Spencer's chocolate-brown eyes pin me in place. "I want that point clear. You, Rylee Everett, are perfect the way you are."

"Bruised knees, sassy mouth, and mad boarding skills included?"

"All the above. And you don't need to compromise who you are to get some guy who is too dumb to notice you without some frilly pink dress." The light turns green and Spencer guns it, switching over into the right lane to get around a minivan going ten miles under the speed limit. "But I know you won't let this drop so—"

"You'll help me?" I jolt forward in the seat, refraining from jumping over to hug the stuffing out of him.

"I'll try. I'm not a miracle worker after all." His stupid smirk is rewarded with a punch to the arm. It might be my last one so I need to get it all out now.

He winces and rubs the spot where I hit him. "Lesson one, guys don't enjoy being hit by girls especially when they can Hulk-smash the hell out of your arm. We do have fragile egos after all. Well, some of us do, and I'm assuming Jax is one of those guys."

"Noted." I lean back into the seat and smile out the windshield.

"You know this is a terrible idea, right?"

My smile widens. "Oh, totally. But aren't most of our ideas?"

"So, where do we start?"

"Galleria Mall. Mom gave me money for summer clothes so I might as well dive into the deep end."

Spencer cuts across the lanes so he can make the freeway entrance. "This is such a bad idea," he mumbles and accelerates fast enough to throw me back into my seat.

I let out a squeak, then break into laughter. This may be a bad idea, but I have one opening and I sure as hell plan on taking it.

7

Spencer

I can't believe I agreed to this.

Rylee chatters nonstop at my side, listing out several stores she looked up on her phone. Six are on our hit list for the day. I've never been in a single one and I can't say I'm thrilled to be doing so today.

I meant what I said in the car. This scheme is ridiculous and I want nothing to do with it when it blows up. Or succeeds. But after last night when my parents sat me down and explained their plan to put the house on the market once summer vacation starts, I knew I had to do something.

Rylee deserves a fantastic senior year. Since my parents can't agree on anything, I might not even be at the same school to make sure that happens. So, the next best option is to find someone who can. Not that I expect that douchebag Jax to be that person, but maybe he's the door to her finding new friends.

My stomach lurches at the thought and I fight back a groan. I haven't mentioned anything to Rylee and I don't plan on it. There's no point in ruining the few months we have left together. If I tell her, she'll get all pouty and that's how the rest of the year will go. Not the memory I want to bring with me to wherever the hell my mom plans on moving.

"In here." Rylee grabs my sleeve and yanks me toward

a store that has a ton of mannequins in some seriously skimpy clothes.

Rylee jumps at the first rack, thumbing through bright pink tops as I hang by the door trying not to gag on the overwhelming cloud of perfume hanging in the air.

"Can I help you find something?" A woman with fire-red hair asks.

In a deliberately slow movement, I check over my shoulder to see who the hell she is talking to. There's nothing but empty space behind me. As I suspected, Rylee already moved on to another rack, her hands loaded down with clothes I never thought she would consider wearing, let alone buying.

Turning back to the sales associate, I force a smile. "I'm good. This isn't really my style." I thumb at a mannequin in a short green dress.

Red laughs, placing her hand on my arm. "I don't know, green might bring out the gold in your eyes."

"Excuse me," Rylee snaps from behind me. "Could you help me with a dressing room?"

Red slides her eyes from me to Rylee then back, a less friendly smile curving her lips as she removes her hand. "Of course."

Rylee wastes no time dumping the armload of clothes at the woman. I swear I'm watching a scene from a movie as she struggles to rein in all the clothing before it hits the ground all while Rylee does nothing to help. Not going to lie, I almost burst out laughing at the woman's expense.

"Good lord, be more obvious," Rylee mumbles once the woman is out of earshot. "They must not take a class on subtlety during orientation."

"What are you mumbling about over there?" I ask and head off in the direction the women went. Rylee planned for five stores and I'd prefer to not drag this out.

"How that chick was all over your junk. I mean, hello, it's a woman's store and they are asking if you need help as I carry armloads of clothes around." Her hand swings through the air and I have to dodge out of the way so she doesn't nail me in the eye.

"First of all, she came nowhere near my junk. Pretty sure I would've noticed that." I reach over and straighten a stack of shorts I knocked over during my duck-and-dodge maneuver. "And second, it probably confused her that I was in the store what with this being chick clothes and all."

"You can't be that dumb." Rylee rounds the corner to the dressing room, shaking her head as I take a seat on an uncomfortable pink couch.

The least they could do would be to get something comfy for the poor souls dragged along to sit around and wait for people to try stuff on. By the time we get out of here, I'll have no ass left.

I pull out my phone as Rylee shuffles around in the changing room, sounding like a raccoon in a garbage can. She normally changes at lightning speed so I'm hoping this pans out the same. Otherwise, I might have to order in pizza with the amount of clothing she grabbed.

Instagram is a bust. Nothing but food and selfies so I move on to Twitter. My thumb slides over the screen as I scroll through the feed, searching for something interesting to occupy my time.

As I scroll past something ridiculous Jax posted to seem *woke* or whatever, I'm struck with a sudden rush of fear. What if this pans out? What if I give Rylee the right pointers and it makes that wiener waffle stop and realize how amazing she is? Then I leave. She's changing herself for him now. What happens if they are in a relationship? How far will she go to keep him around?

"Psst. Spencer." The door to the changing room cracks open and Rylee pops her head out. "I need your help."

"Your head goes into the middle hole."

"Hardy-har." She throws a top that flutters to the ground nowhere near me. "I'm serious. My hair got caught in the stupid zipper. Come help me get it out."

"Why are you always struggle-bussing through life?" Before getting up I glance around to make sure none of the associates are watching, lord knows Red is probably skulking around here somewhere. When I'm confident the coast is clear, I hustle into the dressing room.

Rylee pulls me inside then shuts and locks the door. The room is a freaking disaster with clothes tossed every-where. I sidestep a bunch of hangers and move into the corner that seems to be the only clothing-free spot.

"I guess I snagged my hair in the zipper on the way up now I can't get it down." Rylee spins toward the mirror and scoops her free hair over one shoulder.

Sure enough, a chunk of hair got braided into the zipper. "How did you manage this?" I grab a handful of fabric above her hip and tug her toward me.

"I don't know. Zippers should be in the front. Not stupid backward arm-breaking ones. Who designed them, contortionists?"

I splay my hands on the soft red fabric on her shoul-ders. This girl looks nothing like my best friend. The dress hugs her body like a second skin, making me uncomfortably aware of her curves. Curves she hides under baggy shirts most of the time. Even the wedding dress had nothing on this one.

"How's it going back there?" she asks, fidgeting with the short hem.

The movement draws my gaze down and there goes all the air in my lungs. I've seen her legs before, but not like this. Most of her shorts come down to midthigh. The girl even swims in board shorts. But now her legs are on full display, the toned muscles from hours of boarding flexing as she shuffles her feet.

Our eyes catch in the mirror and I glance away afraid that my longing will bleed right out and make this situation a thousand times more uncomfortable.

"Well, you got it stuck good." I grip the lock of hair and tug on the zipper. "How attached are you to your hair?"

"If you give me a bald spot, I will kill you."

"I make no guarantees." I try the zipper again, this time getting it to move down an inch. Rylee winces but says nothing. We don't have many options here, so I hold my breath and wiggle the zipper down as I pull up on her hair.

It pops loose, taking only a few strands with it. Rylee breathes a sigh of relief as I work the thing all the way down so we don't have another mishap. She scoops the rest of her hair to the side causing the right sleeve to slip off her shoulder.

Too much skin.

Too many bad thoughts.

I take a step backward and scrunch my eyes, fiddling

with the door until my hand finds the knob. "Okay, I'll just be—"

"Wait." The humor in Rylee's voice has me cracking an eye open. "Can you help with the rest? I don't think Jax will go for a bald chick."

My lips pull down into a grimace. I can't handle being in such a small space with her looking all...gorgeous and half-naked.

"I don't have cooties you know." She picks up a skirt from the floor and holds it to her waist. "You can turn around since you seem really squeamish about my bra."

I flinch away. And now I'm picturing her in just a bra. Awesome.

"Bra!" Rylee laughs, reading my reaction wrong. Thinking I'm squeamish about the word and not the image of *her* that comes with it. "How do you date again? I mean for crying out loud, I have way more clothing on than some of the girls you dated."

"It's not the clothes or the..." I wave a finger at her back where I can still see the strap of her polka-dot bra.

"Bra." She laughs harder and turns to face me.

"Right. It's not that, it's—"

"Me?" Her face falls, taking all trace of humor with it. "It's me, isn't it? God, I'm just fooling myself into thinking a change of wardrobe will somehow make me less repulsive to guys."

"No. You look..." I swallow hard, struggling with the best way to phrase my next sentence so it doesn't completely give me away. "You look great. You always look great. I'm just feeling claustrophobic. I...I need some air." My hand swats at the handle, cracking the door open. "I'll meet you up front."

Rylee cocks her head to the side, staring at me as if I've grown three heads. "Okay. I'll be out in a minute."

"Cool. Yeah. Buy that dress. It looks great. I already said that so... Yeah, okay." With that, I slip out and speed-walk to the entrance, keeping my eyes down so no one tries to talk to me.

I wasn't lying. She looked incredible in that dress. If the rest of her purchases are anywhere close, Jax will be drooling at her feet.

I palm my chest over my racing heart as I lean against the railing. Jax doesn't deserve her. He doesn't deserve any of the effort she's putting into this. At most, he'll see her as a conquest, a fleeting hookup. But I know Rylee and once she's set her mind to something there's no changing it.

I just hope she'll be able to handle the fallout once I'm gone.

8

Rylee

My slipper-clad foot taps on the carpet as I examine the clothes I purchased yesterday at the mall.

They're cute and everything, but I'm still not sure how to play this. If I show up to school looking like a different person, it's likely to raise more eyebrows than draw positive attention. But slow and steady puts me on a paper-thin deadline with only a couple of months left before summer break and any chance I have with Jax evaporates.

Gah. I hadn't gotten Spencer's approval on any of the clothes so this could be a catastrophe. He bolted out of the dressing room yesterday acting as if he was being chased by a rabid dog. He said it had something to do with the tight space but I had seen the boy wait twenty minutes in my mother's armoire to scare Ryan.

Yeah. It wasn't the tight space. Not with the way his eyes bulged out when he saw me in the dress. Then there was his reaction to my bare back. He couldn't have been more disgusted. On top of everything, after we left the store, he said his mom called and needed him home.

I collapse onto my bed and run a hand through my sleep-ruffled hair.

Ryan pops his head into my room. "Mom says get downstairs for breakfast." He slips out of view only to appear again. "God, you're a troll in the morning."

The book I throw at him nearly meets his face, but

he moves too quickly, slamming the door and evading the bodily harm he deserves. Okay, so he's right. That isn't the point. He should keep those comments to himself. I don't go around mentioning how he snores so loud I can hear him two doors down with a sound machine on.

On second thought, I should mention it...next time one of his flings comes over.

Notice how I said *fling*? Yeah, he's never had a proper girlfriend in his life. He says he gets bored easily but I'm thinking the girls spend just enough time with him to realize his personality is garbage.

Ugh. Whatever.

I grab the white off-the-shoulder top I bought yesterday and a pair of ripped skinny jeans I've had forever.

Slow and steady wins the race, right?

I run a brush through my hair, making sure all the knots are out before pulling it into a fishtail side braid. Guess I'll have to set my alarm for earlier if I want time to style my hair in those perfect beach waves that a lot of the girls wear at school.

Ten minutes past when Mom serves breakfast, I lope down the stairs and into the kitchen. Will is already gone, meeting the football team before school for some senior breakfast. Mom stands by the coffeepot, reading the newspaper, giving me the opportunity to slip into a chair unnoticed.

"Did Mom give you the wrong laundry basket?" Ryan asks with a mouth full of oatmeal.

"Did Mom give you the wrong food? You're looking kind of pudgy. Might want to skip the carbs," I shoot back as I pull my face into a grimace and reach for a piece of toast.

Ryan's eyes go wide and I have to fight to keep my smile at bay. He's on the wrestling team so weight is everything to him. It's an easy shot I take whenever he's annoying me. So pretty much every day.

He opens his mouth, but Mom sit down in the chair next to me and it snaps closed.

"You look nice," Mom says, reaching for the bowl of fruit in the middle of the table. Her eyes linger on my top where my shoulders are bare, but she says nothing more.

"Thanks." I shovel my oatmeal into my mouth in two disgusting bites then jump up. "Gotta go." I plant a kiss on the top of her head and bolt for the door before she can get any further into this conversation. For crying out loud, I couldn't even sneak a top past her.

Slow and steady is the right decision after all.

Spencer is waiting across the street by his car. He's leaning on the hood, his face turned up to soak in the sun's rays. It's not even summer and the tips of his hair are lightening to a dark gold. By the time we head back to school in the fall, it will be several shades lighter.

When my foot touches the sidewalk in front of his driveway his eyes pop open and find me. "Hey." His gaze drops to my bare shoulders before flicking to my face, a slight frown pulling down his lips.

"Does this look okay?" I smooth the ruffles on my collarbones feeling more self-conscious than when my mom dresses me. When she does it at least I know someone with style had a hand in the choices.

"Looks great." He rounds to the passenger door to open it for me. "Sure Jax will love it."

"Do you think?" I ask once he's in the driver's seat. "It's not much, but I figure it's better than the jerseys and band shirts I normally wear."

"Like I said, he'll love it."

"Are you okay?" I study his face, houses blurring behind his head as he pulls out of the cul-de-sac our houses are in.

"I'm fine." His hand tightens on the steering wheel for a brief second, flexing the leather before reaching for the volume dial.

Then we're drowning in some heavy metal song that makes it hard to think. Forget about talking.

We spend the rest of the ride going deaf from the volume. Spencer doesn't once try to talk once, which is so far out of his normal behavior it's scary. When we pull into a parking spot and the music cuts off, I turn to ask him what's going on, but he's already out of the car and walking toward the front steps.

I grab my backpack and follow. Something is going on, but when he gets like this, there is no point in pushing. Then again, maybe he woke up on the wrong side of the bed. It's rare for him, but I guess everyone has those mornings.

The walk up the front steps fills my belly with butterflies. When I couldn't sleep last night, I plotted and planned. In addition to donning a new wardrobe I decided to at least say hi to Jax. Give a little push to notice me.

I tug the strap of my bag higher, scanning the crowd for Spencer's messy flop of hair. I spot him thanks to his height all the way at the end of the hall heading to homeroom. The butterflies turn to full-blown nausea because

I'm about to do something really stupid and I don't have my best friend as a security blanket.

You can do this.

I make my way down the crowded hall the opposite way of my class toward where I bumped into Jax one morning when Spencer took off with my board. All I have to do is a casual run-by. A friendly good morning. Nothing wrong with that. No clingy stalker vibes because he doesn't know where my first class is. Everything will be fine.

You can do this. You can—

Jax rounds the corner and my eyes bug out of my head. He's walking with a couple of guys from the football team and Haylee, his on-again, off-again girlfriend. Not wanting to chance them being in the on-again phase, I duck my head and pray no one notices me. Getting into a catfight over a guy is the last way I want to start a Monday morning. Or any morning.

Just pass by. Just pass by.

When they're three steps in front of me, Jax's gaze swings my way. His lips tip up into a smile.

I'm so busted.

"Hey, Rylee."

I swear on everything my heart stops. *Someone call an ambulance—I'm going into cardiac arrest because Jax just said hi to me in public!*

My fingers wiggle in his direction totally of their own accord, because my brain is throwing a party complete with heart-shaped banners with Jax's name on them in glittery paint.

His smile widens, crinkling the skin around his eyes

as he swings his attention back to his friends who are busy gawking at me.

And that's where my party ends because as Jax rounds the corner heading for his homeroom, I catch a glimpse of the major stink-eye Haylee is throwing at me over her shoulder.

When I turn down the hallway they came from I lose sight of her, collapsing into the wall. So I've pissed off his crazy popular on-again, off-again girlfriend who is probably on-again judging from the amount of sass she threw. And now I have to wait here until the bell rings because if they catch me going back in the direction I came from it will look weird.

This is why I let Spencer be in charge of stuff like this.

9
Rylee

Spencer hits the rail and grinds, flipping his board at the end just to show off.

We've been at the park for hours, and he's hit some monster tricks, showing off all the skills he's gained and how much better he's gotten over the past year.

Problem is, he's been ignoring me the whole time. With his headphones in, it's as if we're in two different worlds. On a normal day, we'd be goofing off and cheering each other on, but it seems as if he might have a better time if I weren't here at all. That's been his attitude all week, but today it's reached a peak. Which is weird since he offered to give me a ride. Or I guess, I was already at his car and he felt obligated.

Judging from his expression when he saw me, he wanted to tell me to buzz off. Instead, he unlocked the car without a word and waited until I was seated to reverse out. Suppose I should thank him for not turning me into roadkill.

I walk over to the shade where the fence meets grass and collapse under a tree. A group of younger kids have gathered to watch Spencer do his thing. When we're serious about boarding, we've drawn attention a few times. But those are rare occasions. Neither of us is looking to go pro so we do it for fun, clowning around the whole time.

Until today.

Spencer rolls to a stop and pops his skateboard into his hand as Zoe, one of Haylee's BFFs, saunters over, her ponytail swinging in time with her hips. Spencer wipes the sweat off his forehead with the bottom hem of his shirt and graces both Zoe and me with a glimpse of his six-pack.

She sure didn't have eyes for him when he was a gangly fifteen-year-old but now that he's all tall and ripped here she is drooling over him. Gag me.

I glare in her direction as she giggles and pushes Spencer's shoulder. He acts as if she's stronger than she is and stumbles back, rubbing the spot she touched. The whole act has her laughing hard enough for me to hear and from where I sit, I can see a smile lighting Spencer's face.

So, he's not in a bad mood. He's pissed at me for some dumb reason and is too much of a wimp to tell me. Well, whatever. He can stay and flirt. It's not something I want to bear witness to anyway.

Irritation turns to anger, heating my belly with a fire I've never felt before. I've seen him flirt countless times so I don't know what's causing me to get so bent out of shape, but every time Zoe touches him I want to throw hands.

I grab my board and backpack, then stomp away, shouldering past a couple of kids who were watching Spencer's every move until he got sucked in by boobs and a short skirt.

Spencer's bad mood is just rubbing off on me.

But still...I have never wanted to punch someone

more—not even Ryan—than when Zoe put her hands on Spencer.

When I reach the parking lot, I drop my board and take off, dodging a car that's going way too fast. The honk as a result of my middle finger in the air almost blocks out the sound of my name being called.

I stop and turn as Spencer jogs toward me. Zoe is gone, thank God, but the prickly sensation in my gut remains.

"Hey." He stops next to me his board tucked under his arm. "Where you going?"

"Home." I brush a wayward strand of hair out of my face and match the scowl Spencer is sending my way.

"You could have grabbed me."

"You seemed busy flirting with Little Miss Short Skirt."

His scowl morphs into confusion. "Isn't that the look you're going for these days?"

I glance down at the tank top I'm wearing instead of my usual oversize T-shirt. Sure, I have it paired with long board shorts, but again, baby steps. "No. It's not. That would be impractical. I could never skate in a skirt."

Spencer tilts his chin down, fighting the smile bubbling under the surface. "I'd pay money to see that."

"I'm sure you would, perv." I bump him with my shoulder and sigh. "Are you done ignoring me now?"

"I wasn't ignoring you." He kicks a pebble and sends it bouncing across the lot into a ditch.

I flick the earbuds hanging from his neck. "Kinda hard to talk when you have these glued to your ears. Seriously, what's up?"

"Nothing. Just the 'rents…being annoying."

"Heard that."

His nose wrinkles and his big brown eyes find me. "Did you just say *heard that*?"

"Coming from someone who says *lit*. You don't get to judge."

"Well, according to Zoe, the party she's throwing tonight is going to be lit. So, it sounds like you're outnumbered."

My eyes narrow. "Party, huh? Did she invite you?"

He shrugs and heads off toward his car. I pop my board and keep pace with him. Now that he's talking to me I would prefer to have a ride home. "So...did she invite you or what?"

"Yeah she did, but I'd rather stay home and get movie-picking rights since I won the cake bet."

"Um. No. I'm still thinking you had someone on the inside. There's no way you guessed that on your own."

"Don't be a sore loser." He tugs on my ponytail before rounding the front of his car.

I prop the door open and catch his eyes over the hood. "I bet Jax will be there. At the party I mean."

His jaw flexes, popping out the little muscle under his ear. "Okay."

"So maybe we can go? It's been almost a week and I've only managed a quick hello in the halls. If I run into him at a party, I can show him relaxed girly Rylee. Like at the wedding. We are on a tight deadline here. Eight weeks until school lets out."

"Don't remind me." Spencer's eyes cloud over with something I can't quite read, but then he blinks and the moment passes. "I'm not feeling a party. You go. I'm sure he'll be happy to see you."

"What?" I grip the door, the thought of walking into a party to talk to Jax without my best friend there makes me want to puke all over the pavement. "I'm not going alone. Besides, I wasn't the one who was invited."

"So, I invited you and then got sick or something." Spencer slips into the car, slamming the door hard enough to rock it.

I climb into the passenger seat and kneel on the tan fabric, leaning across the center console. "Please. Please. Please." I clasp my hands together under my chin and throw in a little dog whimper noise, one that Spencer can't resist.

He eyes me, taking in my whole pathetic act before groaning, "Fine."

"Yay!" I launch over into his seat and wrap him in a hug, planting a loud, wet kiss on his cheek.

He makes a disgusted sound in the back of his throat and nudges me off. "But, I get two movie selections now. And you will never ask me to go to one of these things ever again because I hate them about as much as I hate soccer."

"Deal." I settle in my seat unable to keep the stupid grin off my face. In a few short hours, I'll be off school grounds in the same area as Jax and can finally get my plan rolling.

10

Spencer

Why am I here?

Oh, right, because I'm an idiot.

I grip the steering wheel a little too hard, turning my knuckles white as I peer at the house at the end of the block that has bodies pouring in and out of the front door. This is the last place I would ever want to be. Yet here I am.

Is there an award for the biggest sap on the planet?

If I hadn't followed Rylee out to the parking lot, we'd be at home, watching a movie and eating our weight in junk food. Instead, I made the dumb choice to skate alone then flirt with Zoe even though there's not a shot in hell I would ever go there. But damn, I wanted one freaking afternoon without the mention of Jax.

That didn't work out.

Rylee sits in the passenger seat, bouncing up and down from nerves. After dinner, she dragged me to her room to approve her wardrobe. Something I will deny until death because no one needs to know I helped her pick out shoes to match that stupid dress she got her hair caught in at the mall.

I should have convinced her to wear her normal getup but I guess that goes against her whole plan. And my plan to ensure she's happy.

Not that Jax will make her happy, but I know better

than to argue with her. She'll double down so really there's no point.

I catch her adjusting her hair in the visor mirror. She spent most of the time before the party curling it after countless YouTube videos. Now it flows in loose waves down her back, begging for my fingers to run through it.

I clench my hands into fists, just in case they have a mind of their own, and tap them on the steering wheel. *She doesn't want my hands on her. She wants Jaxhole.* No clue what she sees in him. I've heard him talk in class. Not the brightest dude out there.

"Are you ready?" Rylee smooths out the front of her dress bringing my attention back to the fact that it hugs every one of her curves.

Jax is such a lucky dumbass.

"Sure." I pocket my keys and slip out into the warm night air.

Music thumps loud enough to reach us a couple of houses down leaving me to wonder how long it will take for the party to get shut down. Sure, we're in a less crowded area than where we live, but still, I can't imagine neighbors wanting to listen to this noise. Praying some disgruntled old lady calls the cops before I have to subject myself to this idiocy.

Rylee links her arm through mine and keeps pace with my irritated strides. Once again I'm reminded that I could be at home watching some terrible B movie that would have Rylee laughing and cuddled close on the couch. Instead, I'm here. *Yay.*

"So, what's the plan?" Rylee asks.

"This was your idea. Figured you had some grand scheme."

She hauls me to a stop, her face paling in the soft moonlight. "I don't know how to do any of this. The last party I went to was mine. And it was you and my family at Sky Zone."

"We don't have to go in there."

"No." She rolls her red shimmery lip between her teeth, a slight frown creasing the skin between her eyebrows. "I want to. I just…"

I place my hands on her shoulders and give them a shake, infusing humor into my voice. "You'll be fine. Pretend your mom is watching from some dark corner. Keep the sports talk to a minimum and laugh at whatever stupid thing he says. Guys like that."

"If that's the case, I should be laughing every time you open your mouth."

"Funny." I release her and turn toward the house. "Now, let's get this over with so I can go home."

"Don't sound too excited." She walks close to my side but keeps her hands to herself.

She's likely worried Jax will see us together and think we're *a thing*. Maybe I should stake my claim, then I won't have to worry about her heart getting broken by some Neanderthal.

No. This is what she wants.

If I keep reminding myself of that, I won't punch him in his annoying smug face. Maybe… Probably not.

Noise envelopes us the second we step into the house. Music is bumping loud enough to shake the walls. People are everywhere, some screaming over the bass. In short, it's chaotic.

Rylee wiggles her fingers at her sides the same way she does every time she's nervous, almost as if she can force the nerves right out of her. I make eye contact and tilt my head toward the kitchen. We can't just stand in the entrance.

Say hi. Get out. How hard can it be?

Rylee's gaze darts around the room no doubt searching for lover-boy. When she's satisfied he's not here, she moves toward the kitchen. I trail behind, noticing a kid from my English class checking her out with all the nuance of a hand grenade. The punk even has the balls to reach out to grab her ass. I'm two seconds away from throwing him through the freaking wall when a girl next to him slaps his face. Hard. I only catch the tail end of the screaming as I pass, but it looks as if Grabby no longer has a girlfriend.

Good.

Rylee's brown curls flow out behind her as she rounds the corner into the kitchen. I'm five steps away when Zoe saunters out, and zeros in on me with laser focus.

"You came!" She yells over the thudding of the heavy bass rattling the frames on the walls. In the next breath, she's all over me, pressing her lean body into mine, and drawing my attention down to the low scoop of her neckline, then farther where a dress should be instead of what appears to be a T-shirt.

Her hand trails down my arm in a zigzag pattern until her hand clutches mine. "Let's grab something to drink." Her lips graze my ear as she pulls me away and drags me toward the kitchen.

No clue why I'm entertaining this. Sure, she's pretty. Most guys would kill for a shot with her, but would it be fair for me to lead her on? Because even as we walk, my eyes search the area for Rylee. It's magnetic. When she's near I want nothing more than to be with her. No amount of legs and tits can distract me.

Zoe shoves a red cup into my hand, leaning close enough for me to smell her fruity perfume. I guess I missed that out in the hall what with all the sweaty bodies grinding everywhere. Here, in the kitchen, it's less crowded, and the music is at a more tolerable volume.

"Seems like it's been forever since I've seen you at a party." Her red-tipped finger dips into the waist of my jeans as she tugs me toward her.

Ballsy move.

"I'm a busy guy... what can I say?" I take a sip of the beer and try not to gag. I will never understand why people like this crap.

"Not too busy for that chick Rylee."

"Never," I deadpan, not caring about the over the top pout of her lower lip. There's no point in sugarcoating it. Rylee will always be first. That's the best friend code.

Speaking of...

I scan the kitchen again, searching for my party companion, and almost choke on a mouthful of beer. She's over in the corner at the dining table, where a rowdy game of poker is taking place. Jax is there. Shocker. And all this would be fine if she wasn't sitting on his lap, giggling like a freaking lunatic.

Beer splashes all over my hand two seconds after I hear the crunch of the red cup I was holding.

Zoe shrieks as liquid leaks all down her white dress. "What the hell?" She rubs at the growing stain, doing nothing but spreading it.

"Sorry." I toss the cup on the counter and stride toward the table, Zoe's cursing fading into the music.

Over the heads of a couple of guys bending down to get beer Rylee's eyes catch mine and widen. *Oh my God,* she mouths and fails miserably at keeping a stupid grin from her face.

I stop dead in my tracks, the air knocked from my lungs. What am I doing? I was seconds away from ripping her off his lap and pounding his face in.

Rylee turns her attention to the game and I take that opportunity to bounce. She got what she wanted but there's no way in hell I can stick around and celebrate with her.

11

Rylee

How did I end up on Jax Lever's lap?

I bite my upper lip and choke down the insane rambling bubbling to the surface. Five minutes ago I was going to the kitchen for something to drink and ran into an inebriated Jax, staggering his way to the keg. Not that he needed any more alcohol judging by how his body swayed while standing still. He took one look at my dress and grinned. Then the next thing I knew, he had hauled me over to a game of poker and pulled me right down. On his lap. His lap!

The only other laps I've ever sat on were Santa's and my dad's when I was a kid. And those times never lifted as many eyebrows. Seriously, several of the guys keep shooting Jax weird looks. One guy asked who the hell I was. Kind of insulting considering he's in my English class and sits two desks up.

Whatever. I got their attention. Yay? This is what I wanted, well, minus the whole lap thing, but it tastes bitter. Loud music. Roaming hands. An audience. Nothing like how I imagined it.

I squirm, trying to find a more comfortable position. Guess I've never spent long enough to realize before, but laps are not the most comfortable things to sit on.

A hand wraps around my waist and tugs me back at the same time Jax leans in. "Keep squirming like that and I'll have to take you upstairs before this game ends."

I freeze and so does my heart. One thump, slam, and then nothing for a solid five seconds. Did he just insinuate that we will be having sex? My gaze flies to the kitchen, searching for Spencer. I might have gotten myself into this mess, but Jax is out of his mind if he thinks sex is on the menu tonight. Or any night in the near future. I'm so not that girl.

Shit, I'm barely a girl at all to most of the male population.

Where the heck is Spencer? My gaze darts around the kitchen, hunting for the mop of hair he can never quite get under control.

Found him.

Talking to Zoe. *Shocker.*

Her and her stupid short dress and perfect face. She's all over Spencer every chance she gets.

I telepathically scream for him, summoning all of our years of friendship vibes. Zoe is talking and getting all kinds of handsy when Spencer's eyes find me...right as Jax brushes a hand over my dumb ticklish knee. I can't help the laugh it causes, but I managed to mouth *Oh my God* and pray he gets the hint.

Spencer turns his full attention to me and boy does Zoe appear pissed about being dismissed. She shouts something I can't hear over the music and stomps off, wiping at her dress as Spencer makes his way through the crowd toward me.

Thank God.

Wanting to catch Jax's eye is one thing, but I never imagined it would be while drunk and horny.

Jax throws his cards down and lets out a cheer, drawing my attention. I see all face cards but no idea what they mean. He's happy so I guess he won?

As he's sliding a pile of chips our way, I turn back to where Spencer was two seconds ago, but he's gone.

Uh, best friend foul.

And that's my cue to dip out. "I, uh, need a bathroom break." I give Jax a pat on the shoulder and hop off his lap, ignoring the snickers from the rest of the guys. Then I bounce before he gets his drunk body moving.

Walking as fast as my wobbly ankles can take, I make my way through the kitchen. When I don't find Spencer, I circle the living room where people are getting drunker by the minute. The game of beer-pong might have something to do with it.

There's an office right off the living room, it doesn't seem to be too popular of a place to hang out, but I try it anyway.

Still no Spencer.

I spot Zoe over by the fireplace with the rest of her friends. She has a giant stain on the front of her white dress and looks about as happy as my mom when I come home covered in scratches and bruises after a long day at the park. Risks of partying, I guess.

I whip out my phone, sliding to the wall where I'm at least a little out of the way. And there it is, a notification from him. Saying he left... Why would he ditch me?

Shoving my phone into the pocket this magical dress came with, I make my way to the front door. It's not even ten, and I'd hardly had any alone time with Jax, but I guess it isn't meant to be tonight.

"Rylee?"

I turn to see a girl from my World History class. She's clutching a red plastic cup and staring at me as if I've up and grown three heads.

Oh. Right. The clothes.

I give her an over-the-top wave before slipping out onto the porch. No way do I want to be roped into explaining my whole metamorphosis. The rollout of the new me might not have been slow enough.

The slight bite to the air has me wrapping my arms around my stomach as I walk toward where Spencer parked. *I still can't believe he ditched me. Not even a goodbye and right when I was sending mad SOS signals that I needed his help.* Then again, he *really* didn't want to come. Suppose this is my payback for dragging him away from his precious movies.

It takes a lot longer to make my way to where he parked than it took earlier, due to the lack of light and a crazy amount of pebbles on the sidewalk. I mean, honestly, did it rain rocks while we were inside? I buckle several times, one of which almost takes me to the ground. Not sure why I came all the way out here when he had a head start, but I hoped he decided to get some air and not abandon me.

My hope turns out to be correct when I spot Spencer in the driver's seat with his forehead resting against the steering wheel.

Best friend status secure. For now.

I whip open the passenger door, making him jump.

"What the hell, dude?" I ask as I slide into the seat and kick off the evil heels in the same movement.

"Rylee. What are you doing out here?"

"I could ask you the same thing. I was sending you a

mad SOS signal back there, and you bounced. What's up with that?"

Spencer's eyebrows scrunch in and he just stares at me for a few seconds. "You wanted me to get you out of there?"

"Duh. Do I look like the type of girl who wants to sit on some guy's lap like a prized Chihuahua?"

"It wasn't some guy, it was Jax."

"Exactly. I don't want to be some drunken hookup. The whole point is for him to notice me and realize how amazing I am. I don't think that will happen with the four brain cells he had working in there." I pull my hair up into a messy bun then slide my leg underneath me so I can face Spencer. "So why did you ditch me?"

His shrug comes as a lazy bob of one shoulder. "I told you I hate parties."

"Well, you seemed pretty into Zoe a few minutes before. Which had me thinking. You're helping me land a guy. Let me help you bag a girlfriend. Not that you would need much help from me. You could literally walk into a room and scream you're single and ready to mingle and at least five girls would come running." And if that means I don't have to see him with Zoe anymore that's bonus points.

Spencer laughs, shaking his head. "Single and ready to mingle? That might get me blacklisted."

"Minor details." I wave off his words and lean my head against the seat. "The point is, I can give you a hand while you're helping me. Then boom, we both have dates to prom and a whole awesome summer. But only if you promise to not ditch me 'cause I don't think I would know how to function without my bestie by my side."

Spencer smiles, but it doesn't reach his eyes. "I've done the dating thing. Now, I want to focus on school and skating."

"Which means continuing to spend ninety-nine-percent of your time with me? I know I'm awesome, but don't you want to—"

"What?" He turns to face me, anger flaring on his normally relaxed features. "Am I not enough for you? Is our friendship some kind of burden? Do you really need emperor Jax to prove your worth? Because I'm positive he's not worth your time if you have to change who you are to get him to notice you."

My mouth drops open from shock. In all these years, I don't think Spencer has ever spoken to me like this. "That's not what I'm saying. You know I love every second with you."

He scoffs and rolls his eyes.

"You're my best friend, but I want more. I'm sick of being that skater girl or just your best friend. I want something I'll always remember from high school. Something to tell my kids. And if that means changing how I look temporarily, then it's a small price to pay. I'll always be Rylee Everett no matter what clothes I'm wearing."

"Yeah, well, the Rylee I know would never sit on some dude's lap while he practically fondled you with a thousand people watching." Spencer starts the car and peels out from the curb, cutting the quiet night with the squealing of his tires.

I sit there in stunned silence as he drives us home. Spencer has been weird lately, quieter than normal, but he's never come after me so hard. Not even when I launched him off a trampoline and broke his arm when we were thirteen.

Something is bothering him, and for once, he doesn't want to tell me. Doesn't want my help.

Ten minutes later he pulls into his driveway and cuts the engine. Before I have a second to speak, he jumps out and slams the door, rocking the car with the force. With a sigh, I gather my shoes and step out, staring at his retreating back.

"Spencer!" He stills, and even in the dim light of his porch I can see his shoulders tense. "Are we still on for the movies tomorrow?"

After a few silent moments that feel longer than an eternity, he shakes his head. "Can't. Why don't you ask Jax or something?" With that, he opens his front door and slams it behind him.

I make my way across the street, my shoes dangling from one hand. My dad's car is still gone. Earlier he took my mom out on a date. They try to do it at least twice a month. It's the reason I figured tonight would be my night with Jax. It was a sign that I didn't have to put up with my mom's interrogation about my dress.

Seems as if the universe had other plans.

I toss my keys into the bowl and dump my shoes next to the ever-growing pile of sneakers piling up by the door. Hopefully, Mom won't notice them in the clutter.

Will pokes his head out of the kitchen as I walk through the living room to the stairs. His eyes travel down my outfit before narrowing on my face. "You're home early."

"Okay?" I continue toward the stairs, but his throat clearing stops me.

"Where's, Spencer?"

"At home." I turn to face him, leaning against the banister as he props a hand on the wall.

"Don't you normally watch movies Saturday nights?"

"Are you keeping tabs on my every move?"

"Just curious why you look like some alternate reality version of my sister. Hot date?"

"When do you move out again?"

He grins and runs a hand through his hair. "Seriously, where were you?"

"None of your business, Dad." I grip the railing and spin around, hoping he gets the point and leaves me alone.

"Heard there was a big party tonight." I stop on the stairs but don't turn. "The least you can do is put the poor kid out of his misery before you go throwing yourself at another guy."

This gets my attention and I whirl around to glare at Will. "What are you talking about?"

He rolls his eyes and sighs as if I'm the dumbest person on the planet. "Be careful with Jax. I'd hate to lose my scholarship a few months before graduation for beating the shit out of him." His phone dings in the kitchen drawing his attention.

He leaves me standing on the stairs confused about what guy I should put out of misery.

As I walk up the front steps of the school, my stomach is a swirling mess of nerves.

I didn't see or hear from Spencer all day yesterday. In fact, I haven't heard from him since he slammed his door on me Saturday night. This is the longest we've gone without talking. The only time in our whole friendship there has been unplanned radio silence.

I've hated every second.

I wipe the sweat off my forehead from the ride over and pin my board under my other arm. Spencer's car was nowhere to be found this morning, leaving me to board to school on my own. Another first. I've ridden shotgun every day since he got his license. That's how I know something is seriously wrong. And him not talking to me about it...well that makes me want to puke.

At least we have homeroom together. He can't avoid me there.

I tuck a piece of hair behind my ear as I walk through the front doors. I was too thrown by Spencer that I forgot I needed to stick with my whole new look. Although, I guess jean shorts and a tank top can be considered girly to some.

Just not to Jax.

And now I feel super self-conscious. I can only pray I don't run into him today.

A few boys I've never talked to before waved at me from the other side of the hall. I throw a puzzled look their way and wave. I've been going to this school for three years and I can count on one hand how many times a boy, hell a classmate, has gone out of their way to say hi. Most of my time is spent in the company of Spencer or my brothers so I guess the intimidation factor must plummet to zero when I walk the halls alone.

Thoughts of my less-better half have me scanning the crowd. I spot his mop of brown hair in the distance headed toward his first class away from me. Hiking the straps on my backpack higher on my shoulders I dodge one of the football players and rush forward in a vain attempt to catch him before he reaches the classroom.

I almost reach him too, but a tall figure with a godly face steps out in front of me, blocking my path.

"Hey, sexy." Jax's lips tip up into a smile and I crane my neck behind me, trying to work out who the hell he's talking to. "Where'd you run off to Saturday?"

Oh shit. He's talking to me.

I clear my throat and drop my gaze to the linoleum, cringing when I catch sight of my clothes once again. "Oh, um. My ride bailed, so I had to duck out."

Jax nods and runs a hand through his thick blond hair. "I don't think I've ever been ditched before."

"I didn't. I mean...you were into your game and I—"

"You can make it up to me. Let me take you out tomorrow night."

My jaw unhinges, and I swear it takes a good fifteen seconds to process what he said. "You want to—"

"Take you out. Tomorrow." His eyebrows bunch

together and I'm positive he must be thinking how conversationally challenged I am.

Before he can change his mind, I blurt out my answer. "Yes!"

The eagerness in my tone brings the smile back to his face. "Cool." He extends his phone and I take it with shaky hands. "Put your number in and I'll iron out the deets with you later."

I managed to put the number in right—despite the tremor racking my body—and return his very expensive phone before I drop it and shatter the thing into a million pieces.

"Catch you later, Rylee." He winks and heads off down the hallway in the same direction Spencer was headed.

Shit.

The bell rings and I cringe. I'll have to grab him after homeroom.

I practically dance down the hallway, floating on the high that is my future date with Jax. Who knew all I had to do was throw on a pretty dress and I would be one of those girls with a boyfriend instead of just the girl with mad boarding skills and a best friend who puts up with my loud mouth.

Speaking of...I walk into class and come up short, almost making the person behind me crash into my back. Whoever it was curses and skirts around me but I'm too busy staring at the back of the room to take in details.

For as long as I can remember whenever Spencer and I have a class together we sit together. Right beside. Right behind. One time a teacher put us alphabetically. It was a sad year. But in all these years, he's never chosen a seat away from me on purpose. Yet, there he sits...all the way in the back with a hood pulled over his head, scowling at the desktop.

Thanks to Jax making me late, there are no other open seats except the one I normally sit in...all the way on the other side of the room toward the front.

I glare in his direction, hoping he can feel my irritation in the depths of his soul but he doesn't so much as glance up. Too enthralled with the landscape of his new desk.

With a growl, I make my way to my seat and throw my bag down, pitching a fit when I see Mike Miller, a giant tool who stuck me with every single project last year when we were lab partners. I haven't spoken to the guy— looked at him—since, and now here he sits.

My back slams into the hard wood of the chair right as Mrs. Green waltzes into the room and the class quiets down. I pull out my phone, despite it being our teacher's one rule, and cradling it in my lap I shoot Spencer a text. His hand falls to his pocket, but he doesn't look. Instead, he reaches into his bag and pulls out our World History book.

Fine. If he wants to be that way, I can ignore him too.

I pop in my earbuds and crank the music high enough to hurt. Then I pull out my homework and go over it all, making sure I didn't miss anything.

By the time the bell rings, I'm still fuming. As I'm putting my stuff away, I catch Spencer jet for the door, taking the long way around instead of cutting through the aisles and walking past me.

Ugh. Whatever.

I head for the door realizing my best friend's crap attitude has snuffed out the excitement of my date. And here I was hoping he would share in my excitement. Guess whatever crawled up his butt and died has something to do with me. Just wish I knew what.

———

The day dragged on so slowly it was almost painful. Spencer never came to the cafeteria at lunch and I never spotted him in the halls. It was almost as if he turned into some kind of superhero with the ability to play the best game of hide-and-seek.

Spencer plus five. Me zero.

I trudge out the front doors and down the stairs, headed for his car. The day may have started with a who-cares attitude, but now I want, no I need, to know what's up. I'm so far gone that I skipped my daily ride around the block so I don't miss him.

Two minutes later as he walks to his car, head bent staring at his phone, my hunch is confirmed.

Crossing my arms, I lean against his door, fighting a smile when he looks up and shock registers on his face. I tilt my head, leveling him with a glare, one I've been using since we were kids.

"Low blow ditching me twice in one day." Spencer reaches for his back door, but I slide over, blocking him. "Still with this whole silent treatment thing? We're not five."

He squints against the sun and runs a hand over his hair, a long exhale deflating his shoulders. "Do you need a ride?"

"That is probably the dumbest question you've ever ask me."

His lips curve up but he rolls his eyes and shoos me with a hand. "Well hop in then. I have dinner with the rents."

Not trusting him, I open the driver side door and crawl inside, climbing over the center console as he stares at me with an adorably confused expression on his face.

"The passenger door didn't break in the past few days," he says as he shoves my left foot out of the way and starts the car.

"I was more worried about how this thing can roll away without me in it." I right myself and reach for the seat belt. "Kind of like it did this morning."

His lips go flat as he reverses out of the spot and into the waiting line of cars. This right here is the reason we goof around before leaving and we still get home at the same time. Today though I'm thankful for it. He can't run away or ignore me if we're locked in a car together.

"So—"

"Just don't." He grabs the knob for the volume control on the stereo, but I slap his hand.

"What the hell is going on? You've been weird since Saturday."

"Do you really care, or do you just want me around for boy advice?"

I reel back. "Dude, are you serious? The past two days have sucked ass. In case you haven't noticed, you're like my only friend. I'm not that friendly."

"Sure seemed friendly Saturday night," Spencer grumbles as he accelerates around a few cars and onto the street, throwing me sideways.

"Did I do something wrong? Because you seem more upset than when I broke your favorite action figure."

"No." Spencer scratches the light stubble on his neck. "My parents are getting a divorce."

"What?" I slap at the buckle on the seat belt not even caring it's illegal and launch over the center console, wrapping my arms around his neck. He curses and swerves, thrown off by my sudden hug attack.

"What happened?"

"I don't really want to talk about it."

His words sting, but I nod and shimmy to my side of the car. "I'm always here for you though. You know that, right?" For a brief second his eyes shift my way, then he returns his focus to driving.

We sit in silence for the rest of the drive. He doesn't even try to turn on the radio—that's how I know this is bothering him way more than he wants to admit.

When he pulls into his driveway, he doesn't bolt like Saturday. Instead, he turns off the car and rests his head on the steering wheel.

"Wanna ditch this family dinner? I can hide you in my closet. Smuggle you food." This gets a small laugh out of him.

"I'm kinda hoping with me there they won't fight."

"Is that why your dad hasn't been home?" He jerks his head in my direction and I shrug. "I noticed his car has been missing."

"They can't stand to be in the same room so Dad has taken it upon himself to remedy that. This is the first thing we've done together in weeks."

Weeks. I knew something was bothering him.

"Offer still stands. Pretty sure you spend so much time over at my house my parents wouldn't even notice."

"Nice to know I have options." He twists and reaches for his bag but freezes when I lay a hand on his arm.

"We cool?"

"We coo." I roll my eyes, which gets another smile out of him. "See you tomorrow, gummy bear."

I grin at my old nickname as I climb out of the car. God, for years that's all he and my brothers would call me. To say I had an obsession with gummy bears would be an understatement. Guess I grew out of that around the time I got boobs and shortly after that the name fell away.

Good to know he remembers stupid stuff like that.

I wave and head across the street as he goes inside his house. My phone chimes as I drop my bag by the door. It's from an unknown number but there's only one person who it could be with a greeting of "hey sexy."

I chew on my bottom lip as another text comes in asking if dinner and a movie is okay for tomorrow night. For some reason, the excitement I felt earlier is gone, evaporated into nothing. More important is making sure Spencer is okay. So, with that in mind, I ask if we can delay the date until Friday. A movie and junk food binge is in order and if it will help Spencer get out of a funk, I'll even let him pick the movies.

"What's the catch," I ask, dropping on Rylee's cushy bed. Today has been a heaping pile of crap loaded onto the disaster that was dinner last night.

My parents made it through appetizers before they were at each other's throats. To say this divorce is bitter would be a gigantic understatement. By the main course, Mom was in the bathroom crying and Dad was pretending nothing happened. Pretty much their MO their entire relationship.

"No catch." Rylee crosses her legs under her and tosses the remote at me. "Pick whatever. The 'rents are out, and so is Will, so we can order in food. Might have to share with the evil twin, but it's a fair price to pay for him to leave us alone."

I try to stop the acceleration of my heart when she mentions us being alone together. We've been alone more times than I can count but hearing her say it does something weird to me.

"So you're saying I can choose whatever movie I want *and* dinner and there's no catch? I'm not buying it, Everett."

"You think so little of me." She sprawls out on the bed next to me, her tank top riding up to reveal her belly button. "Seems you're cracking under the pressure. I have no choice but to revoke movie rights."

"Uh. No." I twist away as she grabs for the remote. "I was just double-checking that we haven't fallen into some alternate reality."

"Fine. Whatever. I draw the line at my pillows." She reaches behind her and fluffs the two propping her up. "And nothing scary."

"This is sounding less and less like my choice."

Her hands fly up in the air then slam down on the mattress. "You're right. But if you pick something scary and I can't sleep tonight you have to stay over."

Again, my heart does a backflip and I smother the sensation with a cough. "How does Chinese sound?"

"Like heaven." Rylee pushes up to one elbow and snags her phone off the nightstand. "Extra pot stickers and sesame chicken?"

At my nod, she places the phone to her ear. "Hey, idiot. We're ordering Chinese want some?" She pauses as her mouth twitches to the side. "I don't care if you're in the mood for Mongolian." Another pause. "Fine, get your own food." She hangs up and turns to me. "Gollum is on his own but I still say we order extra. He's bound to show up and raid us before retreating into his hole."

Her feet hit the carpet with a soft thud, her phone already pressed to her ear again. She paces the small space as she places the order then turns and flashes me a smile. "Want something to drink?"

"Coke is good." As she slips out into the hall, I scroll through the movies.

There are so many titles I've been dying to see that she vetoed, but I pause over a movie I heard was terrifying. I'm not one to watch this crap, most of the time I find it hilarious, but her words keep coming back. I haven't slept over in ages. We must have been fifteen the last time. Right now, with how much my parents are bickering and the way I know Rylee acts when we watch horror movies, it sounds like the perfect night.

By the time she comes back clutching two cans of Coke and a bag of popcorn, I have the film cued up. She takes one look at the screen where I've paused on the opening credits and narrows her eyes.

"What is this?"

I stretch out my hands in front of me. "Let's just say I would pee before we watch this."

The color drains from her face. "Really? This is why I don't give you movie-choosing rights. Out of everything you *had* to pick something scary?"

"It called to me." I pat the mattress next to where I'm propped up on all her pillows. "While the night is young. You don't want to be watching this during the witching hour."

Irritation mixes with fear on her face as she crosses the room to her bed. With a grunt, she throws my soda at me. I catch it before it slams into my face, much to her disappointment. It will be a while before I can drink it now. As I set it on the window sill next to me she plops down, pulling her feet up as fast as she can.

Even after all these years, she's never grown out of the monster-under-the-bed phase. It was a big deal when we were kids. She used to make me check whenever I stayed the night. Over the years it faded away for the most part, unless she was faced with something frightening. Like a horror movie. I still find it so adorable.

I can feel a burning up the side of my face that has me

tilting my head toward her. She's glaring so hard I'm surprised my brain hasn't combust.

"What?" I ask, even though it's giving permission for her to rip into me

"Pick something else."

"Hell no. You gave me two movies which means I pick whatever I want. If that includes demon possession or someone's insides being ripped out for the fun of it then you need to suck it up, my little gummy bear."

"I'm not scared." She tilts her chin up in defiance. "They're just stupid."

"Good to hear because there's a sequel." I hit Play before she can say anything more.

The sudden burst of eerie music makes her jump and scramble farther on the bed. She doesn't even protest the fact that I have all her pillows again. Her warm hands find my arm and she snuggles in so far almost every part of my side is touching some part of her body. Vanilla overwhelms my nose as she tucks her face into my neck, peeking at the screen through one eye even though nothing has happened yet.

She always was a wuss.

Her sudden flinch at a loud noise makes me laugh.

"I hate this," she whines and tucks farther into my side, kicking up my heart rate when her lips brush against my neck. "Do we have to watch this?"

"Yes," I whisper and slide my arm around her body, my fingers resting on the bare skin on her shoulder. "It's not real."

"Tell that to my dolls over there staring at me." Her eyes flick to the corner where two dolls she's had since she was a kid sit on her dresser. Her Grams gave them to her, and she's never wanted to throw them out even though they've been collecting dust since the day she got them.

"Better be careful. They can smell fear."

"Spencer!" Her fist lands in the center of my chest making me cough. "I'm not sleeping in here alone tonight so you might as well tell your mom you ain't coming home."

"It's a school night. Besides, your parents will make me sleep in Noah's old room."

"And you'll sneak into mine like every other time." Her fingers bunch up my shirt as another bang rattles the TV.

"Shh. We're missing the movie."

She falls silent, keeping one eye on the screen while the other is closed and pressed against my neck. Every time there is a loud noise or a jump scare, she curls into me, tugging me close until we are almost one person. Not that I'm complaining. I can feel the swift beat of her heart against my shoulder. Whenever her hand moves, gliding over my chest or arm my own beat races to catch up with hers.

This is all I want. All I've wanted for years. Us together, but without the pretense of a scary movie. I want her to open her stupid eyes and see that I'm the guy she's been waiting for—wishing for. But I guess at this point it's a lost cause. In a few months, it won't matter much. Hell, if she gets her way all my dreams will be smashed in weeks, if not days. I've seen the way Jax looks at her in the halls. He has his sights narrowed in and what Jax wants Jax gets.

I'm so focused on my thoughts, paying little attention

to the movie that when Rylee screams in my ear, it makes me jump and slam the back of my head into the headboard.

My eyes frantically scan the screen, searching for whatever freaked her out, but it's at a lull. The damn characters are standing around talking. That's when I hear her shouting.

"What the hell, Ryan!" Rylee launches from the bed, leaving the side of my body cold.

Ryan stands in the doorway a smirk on his lips as he holds out a brown paper bag. "Am I interrupting something?" For a brief second his eyes flick to me and I don't miss the twinkle. Everyone can see right through me to how I feel about her. Everyone except *her*.

"Jesus, you scared the shit out of me." She snatches the bag from his hand and shoves his chest.

"Since when do you watch scary movies? Last time you had to sleep with a night-light for a week."

"I did not."

"Yeah, you did. I also remember you not being able to get up and pee in the middle of the night."

My choked laughter draws her stink- eye. "Whose side are you on?"

I raise my hands in the air in surrender.

"Get out!" She shoves Ryan again, and he stumbles out into the hall laughing. "Don't I get some of that food?"

"Not anymore." She slams the door in his face but it doesn't cut off his roaring laughter. With a huff, she turns the lock and spins to me. "I have half a mind to eat all this myself. You and your stupid scary movie. I won't be able to sleep at all tonight."

I pat the bed, trying my best to make my face sympathetic. "I'll be here to protect you from big scary dolls."

"I hate you."

"You love me."

"It's a fine line, Hendricks."

My growing smile has one lighting her face. "This is the last time I let you pick a movie. It's *The Fast and the Furious* every movie night from here until graduation."

"Whatever you say, Everett."

The bed dips as she sits on the edge, tucking her feet up as the bag of food lands between us. "I hope you choke on a pot sticker."

"I would just come back and possess one of your dolls. You can't get rid of me that easily."

"You're like an incurable disease. The itchy kind."

I chuckle as I pass her a container of noodles. "Oh, admit you love having me around already. Itch and all."

"If there was a Spencer vaccine, I would take two just in case."

I palm my chest. "You wound."

Rolling her eyes, she shoves a ton of noodles in her mouth. "We should take a trip to Oregon this summer. Check out the college and go camping at Cannon Beach on the way back. Mom hasn't pestered me about getting a job, so if we plan it soon, I can use it as an excuse."

My heart falters at her words. I don't know where I will be living come summer. Mom has been talking about moving home to Washington State. Deep down I know that's where I'm headed.

"Um. Yeah maybe."

Rylee cocks her head, catching the hesitation in my

voice. "What's up? You get weird every time I bring up Oregon lately."

I bob a shoulder, reaching for the container of pot stickers. "Just think we shouldn't set our hearts on it. We haven't even been accepted."

"Please. Will was accepted. That's enough reassurance."

"Let's get through this year first." I shove a pot sticker into my mouth and motion to the screen where the movie is starting to ramp up.

I'm using the movie as a distraction. No way in hell do I want to tell her what's going on. Sure, I broke down and told her my parents are getting a divorce, but that's only because I didn't want to tell her the real reason I had been in such a pissy mood.

We polish off most of the food by the time the movie ends. It's only a bit past nine, but Rylee can't seem to keep her eyes open. Her head lolls to the side, resting on my shoulder. Soon after, her breathing evens out and I sit there watching her chest rise and fall for a couple of minutes, not wanting to move for fear of waking her.

"You should tell her."

I jump at the voice coming from the doorway. Ryan leans against the doorframe, his eyes—Rylee's eyes—bore into me.

"Tell her what?" I shift, letting her head rest on the pillow.

"Come on, dude. The only person who doesn't see it is Rylee, and that's because she is oblivious."

"I don't know what you're talking about."

"Okay. Keep playing dumb. I'm just saying, she deserves the truth. And I'd rather beat the crap out of you for ogling my sister than go after Jax. At least I would win."

I flip him off, which causes him to laugh. The door clicks shut and I refocus my attention on Rylee, making sure she's still asleep. Death would be a better option than having her overhear how I feel from Ryan instead of me.

After a few minutes where I'm certain she's in a deep enough sleep that I won't wake her, I slip out of my jeans, tugging the extra blanket from the end of the bed over me and lay down. If her parents don't know I'm in here they won't kick me out.

For a while I lie there, the warmth of Rylee's body seeping into mine. Ryan's words play on repeat in my head, refusing to let sleep take me. Telling her how I feel isn't an option. I don't want to ruin the last few months we have together. But standing on the sidelines as she runs around with that tool bag Jax isn't how I'd like to spend my time either.

Rylee might have been right the other night. I do need a girlfriend. Maybe that's what I need to break this crush. A distraction. Zoe comes to mind and how gorgeous she looked at the party. She's wanted me for a while now, never subtle in her advances. The way she blows through boys, never settling down for long makes her the perfect person. I can only hope my actions at her party haven't ruined my chances.

With a smile on my face, I drift off to sleep, my thoughts on someone other than Rylee for a change.

Best night of sleep I've had in a while.

Things have been back to normal between Spencer and me this week. Or at least I should say we *were* back to normal.

This morning on the ride to school I told him about my date with Jax tonight and ever since, radio silence again. I saw him once in the hall, but he was preoccupied with Zoe, all his attention directed at her.

Much like right now.

I peek over my shoulder to where he sits with her, an arm wrapped around her as she munches on a carrot. They've been flirty all week. I swear he waits until I'm around to lay it on *thick*. The boy has mad flirt skills when he wants to.

I should be happy for him. After all, I wanted to help him find a girlfriend.

But...

This is one of the few times I've had to sit alone during lunch. The tool didn't even clear it with me first. Had to figure it out on my own when he never showed.

"So, what are your plans for this weekend?" Cora, my favorite gym buddy, asks. She saw me sitting by myself, glaring at an oblivious Spencer, and put me out of my misery.

"Um. Nothing crazy." I choose not to tell her about my date with Jax even though the news would be a bombshell. I don't want word to spread to the whole school. Not that he's been shy about approaching me in the halls. Or his flirty comments. Pretty sure people are catching on.

"Sounds like a blast." She takes a bite of her yogurt and follows my line of sight where I'm once again staring. "Are they dating?"

"Huh?" I whip around my eyes wide because that word and Zoe should never be combined with Spencer. "I don't think so."

"So just screwing around then?"

I glare at her and reach for my chocolate milk. "Did you come sit with me just to piss me off?"

"I came to sit with you because you looked like a lost puppy without Spencer. If stating the obvious pisses you off, you should be thinking hard about why."

"I don't like her."

"Why?"

"I don't know." I toss a piece of lettuce to the other side of my lunch tray. "Her face bothers me."

"You were fine with her last year."

"That was before..." Cora raises an eyebrow. "What are you doing this weekend?" I change the subject because I'm not getting into this. I don't like the girl. As far as I'm concerned, I don't need a reason.

"It's my dad's weekend. So that means awkward conversations and him trying too hard."

"I'll trade you an overbearing mother." Yeah. I slipped and told my mom about my date. She's been walking on cloud nine with a side of smothering ever since.

"I have one of those already, thanks."

"Aren't they the best? It's—" My mouth snaps shut as

a shadow looms over me. Slowly I turn my head, suppressing a squeak when Jax grins down at me, one of his buddies hovering behind him.

"Hey," he says, straddling the bench, his knee bumping into my outer thigh.

"Hey..." My gaze twitches from his friend to him to Cora whose mouth is hanging open in disbelief.

"So, I was thinking we could ditch the whole movie thing." His elbow lands on the table with a thud, fingers dancing across the worn wood. "Malcolm here is having a kickback in the field behind his house. His parents will be out of town so there won't be any interruptions."

No interruptions? I really want to read into that statement.

"Um."

"Bonfire. Music. Come on, Riles." I hold back a cringe at the stupid nickname. I hated it in second grade and I still hate it now.

Flicking my eyes to where Spencer sits, I see he's focused on me even though Zoe's hands are all over his neck and hair. His own hands are clenched tight on top of the tray in front of him.

"Dude, she can't hang."

My attention snaps to Malcolm who is looking more and more irritated by the minute. "No. Sounds fun. Can you pick me up?"

"Eight okay?"

Not the time to tell him my curfew is ten. Maybe I can convince Dad to extend it. "Sounds good."

"You're the best." He winks as he stands and I can't help but notice several eyes on me. One set belongs to

Haylee and to say she looks mad would be an under-statement.

"Uh, what...the hell...was that?" Cora's eyes are glued to Jax's retreating form.

"What?" I ask as I gather the remnants of my lunch. Yeah, I'm not hungry anymore.

"You're going on a date with Jax? How does that fall into nothing crazy category?"

"Because it's not that big of a deal. He asked me out earlier this week. To be honest, I kinda figured he would bail."

"Instead he asked you to one of their bonfires. You're so *in*. Only a select few get to kick back with them."

"Yay me?" I stand and Cora follows.

"Why are you not more excited about this?"

For some unexplainable reason, my eyes slide to Spencer who is busy showering Zoe with all of his atten-tion. "I don't know. Because it's just a party."

"An exclusive party with Jax freaking Lever." She plants a hand on her hip and glances at Spencer. "Does this have anything to do with your hottie of a bestie?"

I trip over the leg of a table, nearly dropping my tray. "Uh...excuse me?"

"Oh, don't pretend you haven't noticed. That boy is a snack."

I cringe and walk away, throwing my words over my shoulder, "Please, never say that again."

Cora catches up with me at the trash cans. "Come on. If he even acknowledged my existence, I would be all over that in a second."

I gesture to where Spencer is once again watching me.

"Well, you got your wish. You might have to fight Zoe for him, but I know for a fact he's single and down to date."

Those words sour on my tongue. Why does the idea of Spencer dating anyone bother me so much lately? Out of everyone, Cora has never been on my bad side. She's the closest thing to a friend, but right now, I want to choke her out when I picture her on a date with Spencer.

I swear lust flashes in Cora's eyes but it only lasts a second before she refocuses on me. "Or you could fight her for him."

"Yeah. Okay." I shoulder my bag and turn toward the doors. "See ya in gym." I race around a crowded table before she can reply.

Spencer and me together is so beyond ridiculous. In the past ten years, he's seen me at my absolute worst multiple times. Puking in a bush after getting sick on the Tilt-A-Whirl at the state fair is enough to squash any romantic feelings for me. And him. After all, it was pink from all the cotton candy we ate.

Students linger in the halls as I make my way to class. This is how far I've fallen. I'd rather show up to class early than watch my best friend grope another girl while he ignores me. And don't even get me started on the discussion about us coupling up.

It's too much for my brain.

"Ry." A hand comes down on my shoulder before dragging me down a deserted hallway.

I spin around, hard eyes killing the attitude I was about to throw Spencer's way. "What's up?" My muscles tense as I scan the hall behind him, searching for Zoe. When I don't see her I smile, but it dies halfway there.

Spencer scowls and takes a step back. "What did Jax want?"

I mirror him, fed up with his weird attitude. "What did Zoe want?"

His nostrils flare. "What does that matter?"

"Oh, I thought we were asking irrelevant questions."

When he takes a step forward, I back up, bumping into the cold wall. "Zoe mentioned lover-boy is having a party tonight. Is that where he invited you?"

"Well, for one, Malcolm is throwing it. And two, it's none of your business."

His hand hits the wall hard enough to make me jump. "Cut the shit. Did he invite you?"

With my heart beating wildly in my throat, I skirt around him. He makes no move to stop me but I catch a slight growl. "I think I'll board home today."

"Don't go to that party. Zoe says—"

"Oh, Zoe says!" I throw my hands up in the air, aware that my voice is rising, but I don't care. He has no right to boss me around. "If Zoe says something, it must be true."

"Rylee, I'm serious. This is nothing like the parties you've been to. You have no idea what they get up to out there."

"Neither do you."

"Which is why I'm not going!"

"Is there a problem here?"

We both stop and shift toward the new voice. Principal Perez stands at the end of the hall, arms crossed over his chest.

That's when I realize how close Spencer and I have gotten. Mere inches separate our faces and with the way we were screaming it's no wonder we drew attention.

"No." I backstep and push a strand of hair out of my face. "Everything is fine."

His eyes volley between us and it's clear he didn't buy my words. Maybe because they lack any conviction. Or maybe it's the way my voice breaks because everything is *not* fine. This tension between Spencer and me...this divide...is a terrible feeling. A knife straight to the gut that just keeps twisting deeper.

"Then get to class."

"Yes, sir." I glance over my shoulder as I pass by Principal Perez. Spencer is standing in the same spot, eyes on me, his chest rising and falling as rapidly as it does after a long day of skating.

And like an ass, I leave him there. Clearly, his parents' breakup is hitting him harder than he let on, but I can't deal with this new Spencer. What he needs is a few days to cool down. When he's ready, I'll welcome him back with open arms.

15
Rylee

Hairspray rains down in a thick cloud making me cough. I wanted to be prepared for anything. After all, it rains here this late in spring every once in a while. This hair ain't moving even in gale-force winds.

Light catches the glitter on my top casting mini rainbows on the wall as I step back to examine my outfit. I've gone all out. Mom knows about the date so there's no point in hiding even though Dad has been grumbly since finding out.

I rub my sweaty palms down the front of the skinniest pair of jeans I've ever wiggled into. They make my legs appear ridiculously long and paired with black wedges I borrowed from my mom gives the impression of curves I never knew I had.

"You look beautiful," Mom coos from the doorway.

I smile and shake my head. This is her dream come true, me all glammed up for my first official date. "Don't think it's too much? I don't want to seem like I'm trying too hard."

"It's perfect."

"Guess those shopping trips you forced on me rubbed off after all," I say, turning to face her and leaning against my dresser cluttered with borrowed makeup.

Something passes in her eyes—pride, maybe. "Where are you going?"

"Dinner and a movie." The lie tastes bitter on my tongue, but there's no way in hell she would let me go if I said we would be hanging out in some field drinking cheap beer.

"Curfew is still ten."

"Got it." I slip my phone into the back pocket of my jeans. It's the real reason I wore them instead of a dress. Guess a purse should be added to my shopping list.

"Here." She holds out a twenty. "Just in case."

"But you already gave me an advance." *Why am I bringing that up? If I don't use it, I can always stash it for emergency board funds.*

"It's not part of your allowance. But don't mention it to your brothers."

I shove it into the same pocket with my phone and check the time. He's five minutes late.

"I'm going to go wait for him outside."

"Wait." She paces a hand on my shoulder as I try to pass. "We need to meet him."

The very idea has me cringing. "Please...don't do this. The whole meeting the parents thing is so outdated. Not to mention embarrassing."

"So, I'm supposed to be okay with my only daughter going out with some guy?"

"Do you meet every girl Will and Ryan date?"

"Well...no."

I shrug and check the time again. Seven minutes late. "Then don't push some archaic rule on me. Get with the times, Mom."

She sighs, seeming to mull it over as the stupid second hand on the clock continues to speed by. I swear if he bails...

"Okay, fine. But if this turns serious, we *will* need to meet him."

"Deal." I plant a wet kiss with a smacking sound to her cheek. "By the way, the guy is Jax Lever. Okay, bye!" I call, then bolt from the room before she can respond.

I checked the weather earlier, and it's supposed to stay warm so I skip the jacket and rush outside. In my house, there's no telling when a brother will be lurking around and having one of them say something stupid to Jax is worse than him meeting my parents.

Once I'm seated on the porch swing my dad built three years ago, I check the time again. Ten minutes. He's ten minutes late. I've never done the whole going on a date thing but I'm thinking it's not a good sign.

Ten more minutes. That's all I'll give him.

As I wait, I push off the ground and let the swing rock. Dad built it for Mom as an anniversary present. For years she kept saying how much she wanted one. My dad being all crafty, obliged and now it sits out here to rot. In three years, it's only been used about twenty times. Poor Dad.

Movement from across the street catches my attention. Spencer walks out to his car, but as if sensing me staring, he glances my way. From where I sit, I can't see his facial expression, but I'm assuming since he hasn't said hello, he's still pissed.

What he has to be pissed about is still unclear. He was the one who agreed to help me win a date with Jax. Granted, it took a lot less effort than I planned for. Apparently, Jax is the type of guy who is easily swayed by pretty dresses. Should have known that judging by his roster of exes.

But still, shouldn't Spencer be happy for me?

After a few minutes of him standing there with his hand on the roof of his car, he turns and jogs across the street.

He's wearing a button-down instead of his normal T-shirt. Even has a nice pair of jeans on. Either he's got another dinner with his parents or a date. His face is blank as he walks up the three steps to my front porch, pausing in front of me.

"Hey." I plant a foot on the ground, stopping the swing.

"Hey."

So...this is awkward.

We stare at each other for a few minutes before he sighs and pushes off the banister. The swing rocks as he plops down next to me.

"You look nice." His gaze travels down my outfit before flashing up to my face. "Seems to me you never needed my help with this whole thing."

I suppose he's right. Years of torturous trips to the mall with my mom must have snuck into my brain and planted seeds when I wasn't paying attention.

I chew on my lower lip, probably messing up the pink lipstick I applied. "I may not have needed your help with this, but I do need you."

Sad eyes meet mine and Spencer nods once. "I just think..." he trails off, crushing his eyes shut, "this is a bad idea—you and Jax. This party especially. You're going to do what you want but I can't sit by and watch you make a mistake."

My heart jumps up so fast and so hard I'm positive I'll have bruised ribs. "What...what are you saying?"

"Maybe we need some space."

"Why does it feel like you're breaking up with me?" My hands twist together in my lap as tears burn my lower eyelids, threatening to wreak havoc on the black liner I rimmed them with.

When I risk a glance up, Spencer is staring at me with...I don't know what. But it's not the same carefree expression he normally wears.

"I would never." He tugs me into a hug and my arms find their way to his neck, pulling him closer. For a second he tenses but then he lets out a harsh breath and melts into me.

"I've hated today. Not talking to you. Not singing at the top of our lungs in the car. I don't think I can do space. Call me selfish, but I need my best friend." New tears spring to my eyes. "If you haven't noticed, I don't have a surplus."

A frown mars his features as he pulls back. "I don't..." A puff of air hits me in the face as he lets out a rough exhale.

"You're my best friend, Spencer. I have a feeling more is going on than you not wanting me to go to a party with Jax. So spill." My fingers slide through the hair on the back of his neck and I realize we're still holding onto each other, but leaning away so we can meet eye-to-eye.

"My parents suck."

I fight the smile simmering under the surface. "Okay, that's a start."

His return smile is forced, dripping with sadness. "They used to at least pretend to love each other, you know? Now it's constant bickering. It's unbearable." His full bottom lip slips between his teeth and he looks as if he might say more. Instead, he sighs again. "I still don't like you going with Jax though."

"Come on. I can't cancel now. I already pushed the date back because you seemed like you needed me."

His stupid frown is back. "When?"

"Our movie night."

"You actually ditched Jax to be with me?"

"I mean, I wouldn't call it ditching. We rescheduled, which is why I can't bail now. Really, me going to this party is your fault."

He laughs so suddenly it catches me off guard and makes me jump away from him. A chill works through my body at the places where his hands once were.

"You're blaming me for having to go to some shit party?"

"Right. So you have no one but yourself to blame."

His answering grin makes me smile. "I suppose I can let the party slide if you promise you're all mine tomorrow."

Butterflies dance around in my stomach at his words. Or maybe it's how he said them. In any event, they do not belong in this situation. This is Spencer I'm talking to for crying out loud.

"I think I can make that happen."

A car honks from the curb by my mailbox. We both turn as the passenger window rolls down and Jax leans over to wave.

"My chariot awaits." I reach over and ruffle Spencer's hair as I stand.

He catches my wrist as I go to pull away and rises until he's hovering over me. "Call me if you need anything. And I mean anything, Everett. I don't care how late."

"Yes, Dad." I wink as I skip down the front steps.

I can feel Spencer's eyes on me the whole time, a heavy weight almost as if I'm doing something wrong settling in the pit of my stomach

When I get inside the car and Jax smiles at me, those butterflies from earlier are nowhere to be found. Not a single flutter. My attention shifts to the stereo for fear of him seeing the apprehension on my face. That's when I notice he's almost thirty-five minutes late. I'd been glued to my phone wondering where the hell he was but the moment Spencer showed up his tardiness was flung right out of my mind.

My gaze swings to my porch as Jax pulls away from the curb. Spencer is still standing where I left him, eyes following the car until I lose sight of him.

Why all of a sudden do I feel as if this date is a huge mistake?

By the time we reach the party we've covered every small-talk topic known to man. To be fair, I might not be giving Jax much to go on. Ever since we hit the freeway, a sick, twisting sensation settled in my gut and the farther we drive the worse it gets until my insides cramped and every turn we make threatens to bring dinner up.

Jax wastes no time jogging over to his friends the second he's out of the car. I spot Malcolm in the mix, giving him a fist bump as his gaze flits to me. Nothing about his face screams friendly.

Yeah, I don't think he likes me much.

I hang back, taking in the gathering of people as they huddle around a massive bonfire and sip on beer being pumped from a keg. It's not as loud or crowded as the party Zoe threw, but I'm still so far out of my element.

Terrifying. A few girls stumble past me, giggling and catching themselves on a rock before righting and continuing on their merry drunken way.

Barely nine and people are wasted.

I kind of wish I'd listened to Spence. Without a wingman, this is overwhelming. I don't know what to say. To do. But I guess standing at the edge of the field like a weirdo while everyone else has fun is the wrong thing.

As I trudge over to where Jax is laughing with his

friends, it doesn't escape my attention he didn't motioned me over. Or acknowledge me since we rolled up.

I force a smile as Jax swings his gaze to me. What I want to do is scream, "*Yeah I'm still here, you idiot.*"

But I don't. I'm supposed to be cool, relaxed Rylee. Going against all of my instincts, I bump him with my shoulder and amp up the smile.

"Riles." Jax throws an arm over my shoulder and tugs me in close, almost spilling his drink down my new shirt. "I was just telling Malcolm that we lucked out he had his party this weekend. We almost had to sit through some chick flick."

Yeah. Lucky...

"Thanks for inviting me," I grit out.

"I didn't." With that Malcolm turns to one of the other guys I'm pretty sure is on the football team who is having a hard time controlling his laughter at my expense.

"Do you want something to drink?" Jax asks, seeming to not notice his friend's rude comment.

"Whatever you're having." I'm not a big drinker, but I don't want to look more out of place than I feel. Plus, how strong can beer be? Jax tugs me over to where the keg is. Haylee's face in the crowd catches my attention and I almost nosedive right into the dirt. It's not a shock that she's here. It's shocking the way she is trying to stink-eye my head into a gory explosion.

Poof. No more Rylee to distract Jax from her.

Jax catches me with strong hands on my hips and rights me. I let out a nervous giggle and try not to focus on the fact that his fingers wander up to my ribs as he walks me the rest of the way to the keg. I also try not to notice that instead of feeling excited that he's touching me, I'm a little icked out.

"Beer for my girl here," Jax says as he plants a soft kiss on my neck and my eyes flick to Haylee.

Yup. Still wishing for my death.

After an awkward stare-down, she flips her black hair over her shoulder and stalks off, her two besties close in tow. Zoe is missing from the gang, which I guess is a good thing.

Unless she skipped the party to be with Spencer...

A sharp pang shoots through my stomach.

I shake it off and take a sip of the beer I'm handed. Why do I care if Spencer is with Zoe? It's been forever since he dated. I should be happy for him. I *am* happy for him. I just need to—

Jax plants another kiss on my neck, lower this time where the fabric of my shirt slipped off my shoulder. I freeze at the contact, the guy who handed me the beer cocks an eyebrow and smirks making what's happening feel that much dirtier.

I spin around, knocking Jax back a step and take another drink. Jax doesn't seem fazed by my attempt to move away from him. In fact, the motion almost seems to encourage him.

He covers the distance in a few steps, wrapping me in his arms when I try to wiggle backward again. I don't know why I'm acting like this. Being in his arms has been a dream of mine for years. And he's doing it in front of all the most popular kids at school. But maybe that's why it feels so gross. It's as if he wants attention. Wants everyone including Haylee to see. My eyes automatically search her out, but I don't find her in the crowd.

"Did I tell you how gorgeous you look tonight?" Jax whispers in my ear, his hands sliding lower until they rest on my lower back a tad too close to my butt.

"No. We were too busy discussing weather and summer plans." I take my third sip of beer. My limit for the night. Need to toss this out. No way in hell I want to get plastered out in the middle of nowhere.

"Well, you do." His lips find my neck again like a damn heat-seeking missile. "These jeans..." His hands sink into my back pocket and there is definite gropage.

My heart flies so fast into my throat I almost choke on it. *Holy shit.* Jax is grabbing my ass as if it's no big thing. As if I go around letting guys put their hands all over me.

I take an unsteady step back, cursing myself for wearing heels when I almost trip. Jax's hands fall to his side and he's staring at me as if I told him I think the world is flat.

"I, uh...have to use the bathroom."

Jax motions to a patch of trees twenty feet away. "Have at it."

"I..." *What?* "You want me to pee outside?"

"Malcolm doesn't let anyone in his house. Party rule." Jax shrugs and polishes off his beer. "Want another?"

I glance down at my half-full cup. "No. I'm good."

"I'm going to go grab another. Hurry back with your fine ass."

My head nods meanwhile my brain is screaming, *What the hell?*

As I walk toward the trees, I check my phone. Shit. It's almost ten. He was so late picking me up I didn't even stop to think how little time that would give us. Judging by his party mentality, I don't think he's game for leaving so early.

I chew on my lip as I lean on the rough bark of a pine tree. I don't have to pee, I just wanted to get away from the situation. This whole plan of capturing his attention went from zero to one hundred in the blink of an eye. I'm so not prepared for everything I assume he expects from the girls he dates.

For crying out loud I've only kissed two boys. One of whom was the result of an unfortunate game of 'seven minutes in heaven' that ended with a black eye when Billy Thompson tried to grope my boob.

Yeah. He never talked to me again after that and ended up moving to another state the next year.

But Jax...I tap my phone on my forehead. I just have to get him alone on a normal date. Once I get to know him better, I'm sure all those butterflies will come and his hands on me will be the only thing I want.

When I reach the outskirts of the bonfire, I see Jax by the keg with Ava Rossi all up on his junk. Freaking hyenas. I couldn't have been gone for longer than five minutes.

I trudge over, clutching my phone in a tight fist because Jax doesn't appear bothered by the grinding this girl is doing on his crotch. In fact, he has a smug air about him.

Just an everyday occurrence for Jax Lever. I stop dead in my tracks, taking in the rest of the group as they seem to pair up making out and groping all over the place. Spence might have been right about this. Totally not my scene.

Before Jax sees me, I slip away, heading out toward

where he parked. I scroll through my contacts until I find his name.

Even though I know he will rub in the fact that he was right, I push the call button. He picks up on the first ring.

"Can you come get me?" I ask before he speaks.

"I'll be right there."

17

Spencer

I find Rylee pacing between two cars. She keeps tapping her phone on her palm and glancing behind her at the faint glow of the bonfire.

If Jax did anything to her...

Her attention snaps toward me when the headlights from my car flash in her direction. There isn't a moment's hesitation before she's jogging to where I park where the trees give way to an open field.

"Sorry if I woke you," she says the second the door is open. "Didn't want to call Will because I would never hear the end of it."

"What happened?" I ask when her butt hits the seat.

"Tell you on the drive. We're cutting close to curfew."

Nodding, I pull out on the darkened street, but I can't stem the worry that something bad happened. When Zoe told me about the stupid party yesterday morning, I knew nothing good would come of it.

Hookup party. That's what Zoe called it. No wonder Jax invited her.

After reaching the main road I shoot a glance at Rylee who was busy twisting one of the silver bracelets on her arm around and around. The silence is oppressive. Suffocating. I can't take it anymore.

"What happened?"

"I don't...know."

What? "Something obviously happened because you called me to pick you up instead of having lover-boy take you home."

She glares at me and after a deep breath, pivots in the seat, tucking one leg under so she can face me. "Let's just say it was the weirdest party I've ever been to."

I swear if she doesn't explain I'm going to flip out.

"It started off fine. We showed up. People drank. Malcolm doesn't like me but that's...whatever. But then Jax got super handsy, much to Haylee's irritation." She flicks a curl over her shoulder and reaches out to fiddle with the temperature knob. "What's up with that, anyway? They break up and hook up more than people in soaps. It's as if she considers him as property. I'm surprised she didn't pee on his leg so—"

"Rylee!" I grip the wheel so hard the leather flexes. "What made you call me?"

"Right." She slumps into the seat, resting her head on the window. "So, he gets all handsy and I freak out because...hello, I've had one boyfriend and I'm not much into PDA. So, I bail and say I gotta pee and this dude points to a tree." She catches my raised eyebrow. "Yeah. He expected me to pop a squat. Thankfully I didn't actually have to go. So I take a breather and when I come back everyone is grinding and sucking face and I see Ava going to town on his crotch. So I called you."

"He brought you and hooked up with another girl?"

"Well, I didn't stay long enough to witness the act, but yeah, I'm assuming."

"You seem very chill about this."

She shrugs and reaches to undo the straps on her

shoes. "We're not official. Technically he can do whatever he wants."

This girl...

"So you're totally fine?"

"Better her than me. I've never been into the whole voyeur thing. Getting it on in the middle of the field isn't really my style."

"So what now? Are you still going to see him?"

She huffs a laugh. "First, he would have to talk to me again. I came with him, then bailed without a word. Again."

Warmth fills my chest in calming waves. She bailed on her date with a guy she's had a crush on for years and the first person she thought of was me. Of course, I would prefer her not dating anyone *but* me, but beggars can't be choosers.

"You think he'll notice you left?"

Her fist collides with my shoulder making me swerve into the left lane. "Dick."

"I'm just saying. Has he even texted you?"

She flips her phone in her hand and lets it land face down in her lap. "No."

"So, are you ready to call quits on this whole make Jax plan?"

"I don't think I'll have a ch—" Her phone rings in her hands, filling the small space with an annoying pop song. "It's him!" She holds up the phone up to my face. "Shh! Hello?"

I try to remain calm. Him calling means nothing. He could be calling to chew her out for ditching him. He could be calling to say he never wants to see her again because he's scum who only wants in her pants.

She giggles.

My heart plummets to my freaking knees.

"No. Don't worry about it. My mom is strict and when she says jump, I do it."

Her laughter fills the cab again and I've never wanted to run into a wall headfirst before, but I'm certain it would feel better than sitting here listening to a one-sided conversation that has her giggling like a crazy person.

"Okay. Yeah. Text me tomorrow." She hangs up and pumps her fist into the air. "He didn't hook up with Ava and has been looking for me for the past fifteen minutes." She hugs her phone to her chest and sighs. "Said he was afraid a mountain lion got me."

"Great." I stretch my neck to the side and try not to give in to the urge to drive right into the lake.

"He wants to take me to dinner tomorrow. Just us. No party pop-ups."

"So...your plan is back on?"

"Duh. Did you hear me? He didn't screw around with Ava. If he had, I would seriously reconsider, but he didn't, so I can continue on with the next step in my plan since he's obviously already noticed me."

"And what's that?" Even I can hear the anger in my voice so Rylee must be on another planet because she just smiles.

"Make him fall for me and score an invite to senior prom."

"Prom? Didn't you say it was for suckers who need constant attention and praise?"

"No, you did, I agreed with you. At the time." She's back to glaring at me. I don't see it because I'm keeping my eyes forward, but I can feel it. "Can't you be happy for me?"

"Do you want party poppers?" I pull off the freeway, thankful to be masked in darkness as I leave behind the ever-present lights lining the road.

"No, but some helpful advice would be nice. As you so sweetly mentioned, I've had one boyfriend that lasted a fraction of a second. We never even went on an actual date. You however have." She pokes me in the side and groans. "I don't want to bomb this."

"Then don't go," I mumble, which earns me another punch on the arm. This is pure torture. "Fine. Be interested in what he says but not overly interested. If he talks sports, go with it but don't let him know your knowledge is on par with his. He seems like the kind of douche who could be easily intimidated by a girl knowing or doing something better than him."

I glance her way to see her chewing on her lower lip in contemplation. "So, don't be how I am with you." She blows a strand of hair out of her face. "I can do that."

"But you shouldn't have to." I throw up my hands as I park in my driveway. "Just felt like it needed repeating. No need to hit me again."

She scoops up her shoes from the floor. "Thanks, runt." She boops me on the nose, giggling at my old nickname. One she used all the time when I was smaller than her. "I'll tell you how it goes."

"Can't wait," I grumble as she shuts the door.

How did I get here again? Oh, right, I'm stupidly head over heels for my best friend who wouldn't notice even if I waved a giant flashing sign. And because of that, I've been lured into being her teacher, all so another guy, who doesn't deserve her, can use her until he gets bored. His motives are crystal clear to everyone but her.

The freaking cherry on this crap sundae is being ditched for that turd after promising tomorrow to me.

Rubbing my eyes, I make my way to the front door, only noticing my dad's car parked next to my mom's as I'm twisting the knob.

As if tonight couldn't get any worse...

Muffled words float to me as I click the door shut as quietly as possible. The last thing I need is some parental lecture about being out past curfew. For two people who have been so caught up in their own drama for the past month, they sure know how to jump in and try to parent when they want to.

I skirt around the corner, taking the long way through the kitchen hoping I can sneak up the stairs without them seeing me. Or, at the very least, play it off as if I'm grabbing a snack. As proof, I snag an apple on the way.

So far so good. I press my back into the wall and peek around the corner. My mom is sitting on the couch, one leg tucked under her and facing my dad who throws his hands up in exasperation. He's mastered that move after all the fights they've been having.

I'm about to make my move and bolt up the stairs when my mother's words reach me.

"We promised we would wait until summer."

My heart jolts in my chest knocking all the air from my lungs and halting my movement.

"It's not fair to make him start a new school with a few months left in the year."

"And it's not fair to hover in limbo," my dad snaps back. "I'm paying a mortgage here and I'd like to move on with my life. We sell the house and you can move back home and I can buy my own place. I'm wasting money at the hotel."

"Then rent an apartment. We have his grades to consider. I'd like him to get into a good college and do something with his life, unlike me."

"Oh, your life is so bad. The moment you found out you were pregnant, I stepped up. I paid for rent. I made sure we lived in a great neighborhood. You could have gone back to college when he started school, but you were complacent. So don't come at me with your jabs."

My foot hits the bottom stair, the same stupid creaky one I learned to avoid when I was thirteen and prone to sneaking out. Both sets of eyes swing my way. My mother's widen in shock and my father, he simply scowls.

"Spencer," My mom says as she stands, flattening down the front of her blouse. "I thought you were in bed."

"Got hungry." I wave the apple in the air as proof, feeling about as numb as the moment they told me about the divorce.

They want me to move now...even after our talk. This is Dad's doing. We've never had the perfect father-son relationship. As I got older, I figured out it was because he thinks I ruined his life. I guess having a kid at eighteen can do that, but shit, it's not as if I had any say in the matter.

"Oh, well, your father and I were just—"

"Discussing how you plan to uproot me midyear," I cut her off, squeezing the damn apple so hard my hand aches.

"No. Of course not."

"I heard you." I swing my accusatory glare toward my father. "Do you hate me so much that you can't give a little?"

To his credit, the scowl lessens, morphing into his normal everyday glare. The same one I wear.

"This isn't about you," he snaps and stands.

"Yes. Yes, it is. Every single decision you guys make right now affects me. And guess what? I'm over it. Get your shit together because I'm not moving midyear. If you want to go at each other have at it, but leave me out of it." I stomp up the stairs, trying not to revel in the shocked expression on both of my parents' faces.

This is the first time I have ever fallen short of being their perfect son. And it felt good. The slamming of my door rocks the photos on the wall. Photos of Rylee and me through the different phases in our lives including one misstep where I thought I was emo.

That lasted a week.

I fling myself onto my mattress and stare up at the ceiling. Mom won't say anything tonight, not with Dad here. But I'm sure I'll hear about it tomorrow.

That is if I'm home...

I dig my phone out of my pocket and shoot Zoe a quick text. She's been practically begging to go on a real date this week. It's time I let loose and just have fun. If my time here is even shorter than I planned for and my best friend is so wrapped up in winning over some douche, I might as well use every moment I have to the fullest.

Starting with taking a hot chick on a date.

18
Rylee

To my surprise, Jax is on time.

I had been banking on him being late what with the whole half an hour I waited on the porch yesterday. That's what left me behind schedule and what gave Mom the opportunity to answer the door.

Not ideal.

Even more surprising is the red rose he hands me as he flashes a megawatt smile at my mom that leaves her giggling and cooing over how great we look together.

Yeah. I got him out of there as fast as possible. Didn't even finish curling my hair. Guess that's what bobby pins are for.

I did, however, have time to notice Spencer's car missing from the driveway. Both of his parents' cars were there though.

"What are you in the mood for?" Jax asks as he speeds on the freeway.

Burger. Fries. Steak. "Whatever you want."

"Really?" He shoots me an incredulous look. "Most girls I date are all about salads. They wouldn't dare let me pick the place for fear of being stuck with something greasy."

Crap. Five minutes in and I'm already failing.

He must sense my panic because his face lights with an easy grin. "I like it. What about Yard House?"

I shrug. I think I've passed it a few times but never been. Spencer and I are into the whole fast and greasy thing. Easy-peasy.

My nose wrinkles when I realize my thoughts bounced to Spencer and aren't focused on the gorgeous god sitting a foot from me.

"Yeah. Sounds good."

"They have lettuce wraps if you're not into the salad thing."

My smile is tight and a bit too enthusiastic. Is he going to flip when he realizes I can eat him under the table? Then again, showing my true colors comes after him falling head over heels for me so maybe he'll think it's adorable.

Spencer sure did when he bet he could polish off more wings at Bdubs back when they still had their wing night. I might have been groaning from pain after finishing forty-two and had sauce smeared all over my face, but he just wrapped me in a tight hug that almost made me puke and told me dinner was on him for the next month.

Twisting my lips to the side, I focus on the blurry scenery outside. There goes Spencer popping into my head again. *He's my best friend. Of course, he thinks all my weird and gross behavior is funny.*

"What do you think?"

My head whips toward Jax. He was talking and I'd zoned out. Now how do I play this? If it was Spencer, I would just admit that I was ignoring him and we would both laugh. I get the feeling Jax won't react the same way.

Do I agree?

Crap. I haven't said anything for a long time.

I can't ask now.

It's been like five minutes since I spoke.

Agree. Go with agree.

"Yes."

"You think your parents will be okay with that?"

Uhhh... "Sure?" I wince when I hear the hesitation in my voice.

"I should invite Will, but I don't think he would appreciate me all over you once I catch sight of you in a bikini."

All the blood drains from my face. What the hell did I agree to and why on earth does Jax think I would *ever* be in a bikini in front of him?

No need to mention I bought one and it's been shoved in the back of my closet ever since.

"Where at?" Innocuous. Unless he mentioned it already.

"Lake Tahoe. It's my grandparents' lake house but they haven't been up there in years. Will be nice to use it before I ship off to Oregon."

He wants me to go to a lake house? Yeah, my parents will *not* be okay with that. Spencer's parents are the only people I'm allowed to travel with besides my own family. And alone with Spencer on rare occasions.

It's okay. Perfectly okay. I'll just tell him at a later date I got grounded or something. Better yet, that my dad won't let his little girl go off with boys. Which is the truth.

But will it turn him off dating me?

"Ready?"

I blink a few times, taking in the restaurant in front of us. Good lord, if I keep zoning out he's going to think I'm on something.

"Yeah. Starving. Let's go get some of this delish food you mentioned." I hop out of his car, bouncing on the balls of my feet and mentally kick myself for sounding spazzy.

Either Jax is used to this type of behavior or he doesn't care, because he drapes an arm over my shoulders and leads me to the front door.

By the time we step out of the heat and into glorious air-conditioning, my heart rate has settled down and I'm certain I can make it through this date with no more idiotic slips.

"Hi there." A gorgeous redhead greets us. Well, greets Jax. Her eyes haven't once moved from his face since walking up to the podium. I never knew what undressing someone with eyes meant until this exact moment.

"Two." Jax flashes that grin of his and I swear the entire restaurant hears her swoon.

Hop in line, chick.

She picks up two menus and leads us toward the back of the restaurant. With her eyes on Jax the whole time I'm amazed she doesn't run into something. It would have made for a comical sight.

Alas, we arrive at our booth with no face-plants.

Miss Flirt leans over the table, placing the menus in front of Jax while also giving him a flash of her cleavage. To my disappointment, he sneaks a peak—okay, ogles— before meeting her lusty gaze and winking.

Ugh. Gag me.

Once we're alone, he slides me a menu acting as if that didn't just happen. Is this how all guys act? Am I supposed to ignore it? I don't remember John, my one and only boyfriend ever, acting this way. Then again, we were fourteen so...

Not wanting to appear extra clingy on our first real date, I ignore it, turning my attention to the menu and all its yummy food.

My gaze stops on the street tacos and I almost let out a whine. Tacos are my favorite, but with all the spices... well, I don't want to risk bad breath. Nothing will ruin the chance of a second date quite like stank breath before a kiss. At least, that's what Ryan says. Since he's the king of making out, I take the advice at face value.

I'm not eating a salad though, so I opt for a turkey sandwich.

The waitress comes and takes our drinks. She at least has the decency to not drool all over Jax but that might be because she's at least fifty.

When she comes back, I let out a sigh. I swear we've been silent for forever. Never in my life has this much time passed where I wasn't saying something. It's part of the reason my mom gave in and stopped going to church. You get way worse dirty looks when talking during a church service than at a movie theater.

"What will you have?" The waitress asks.

My stomach screams for tacos, but I stomp down the demand. "The turkey club, please."

She jots down my order then turns to Jax. "And you?"

"Vampire tacos."

I might cry.

The waitress scoops up the menus and leaves us in unbearably awkward silence. Really. It's way worse than the time my brother Noah forgot he had his webpage up on some...ahem, self-pleasure enhancement page and let Mom borrow his laptop.

Dinner was beyond awkward that night.

But sitting here, not saying anything while both of us scan the restaurant instead of making eye contact is a million times worse. My fingers tap the table and I feel nervous babbling rising to the surface. Which will only make the whole situation worse.

After what feels like a literal eternity, I can't take it anymore. I clear my throat and throw out the first thing I can think of.

"So, are you going to play ball in college?"

Yes, I know, not a topic I'm supposed to dive into. But I can play dumb, right? Let him lead the conversation.

His eyes light up and he bobs his head. "Yeah. I didn't get a scholarship or anything, but I plan on trying out."

"That's awesome. I think my brother Noah played his freshman year at Baylor. I've never been to a game though."

Lie. I went to every game when he played in high school.

"You've never been to a game? Like ever?"

"Nope. I don't get it and no one has ever taken the time to explain what I'm watching."

Lie. Lie. Lie.

"You have to go to at least one game before you graduate!" Jax takes a sip of his soda. "Maybe when I'm down on break, I can go with you. Explain what's going on."

"I'd like that." I spin a curl around my finger and tilt my head to the side. I feel super dumb, but I read about this flirty move in a chick magazine my mom had. Something about exposing the neck.

It made no sense. But whatever. Jax hasn't shifted his attention off my face so it must be working.

Our food comes right as Jax launches into the specifics of his role as running back. I nod and ask obvious questions, staying away from in-depth questions like stats because that will give me away.

Silence is replaced by easy chatter, but I still find myself fidgeting with an odd sensation in the pit of my stomach.

Within an hour we've covered everything from his glory days as a Tiger's golden boy and his plans for college—business major to appease his dad. Yet he hasn't asked a single question about me. Even when he finishes his meal and switches to my side of the booth to slip an arm over my shoulder and steal the fries I had been trying not to scarf down.

"Do you have to be home right away?" Jax asks and scoops up my last fry.

I shelve my death glare and force a smile. So what if this isn't how I imagined our first date would go? It's probably my fault for being so nervous. "Not right away. My curfew is ten."

"Want to go to play some mini golf? I can show you how."

My fake smile actually hurts at this point. Not only do I know how to play, but I'm also the reigning champion in my house. Ryan won't even go anymore. Spencer never seems to mind a beatdown though.

"You'd really show me how?" I bat my eyelashes even though a gag is hovering right there in my throat.

Truth is, I could show him a thing or two. But I'm not supposed to be that Rylee. The girl with mad boarding skills and a bit too much competitive flare. Guys don't appreciate that. Seventeen years have proven it.

"It will be my pleasure." His finger skims over my hand and I wish for butterflies. A spark. *Something*. But all I feel is tension and pressure to be the girl I'm not.

For now. I just have to keep reminding myself that my act is just for now.

"Can't wait."

Jax lifts his hand in the air as he signals the waitress. There is no hesitation as she sets the receipt down and speeds away to another table. I reach for my purse right as Jax pulls out cash.

His smirk is a little over the top as he slips some bills into the little black check holder. "I got this."

Why is it when he says that I want to punch his smug face but when Spence says the same thing it makes me smile? Maybe because I always pay him back. As I slide out of the booth, I decide I'll be paying for mini golf. Whether or not he likes it.

Jax walks by my side as we head for the front doors. Out of the corner of my eye, I catch him wink at the hostess, causing her face to flame as red as her hair and have a fit of giggles tumble from her lips.

The moment we step outside, Jax snags my hand and links our fingers.

Nothing.

Dead air in my stomach.

Not even a slight flutter.

The short ride to the arcade and mini golf course has my nerves on high alert. This is all I've wanted for years. What in the world is going on? The sight of Jax in the halls used to send my heart tripping over itself and now, nothing.

Nerves. It's got to be nerves.

I wipe my sweaty palms on my legs as I get out of the car. For a Saturday the place is dead. Which I suppose is good. It will give Jax time to "show me how to golf," which is really an excuse to have his sexy arms wrapped around me.

Jax beats me to the counter and pays for the game before I even pull out my wallet. I smile as he hands me a club but I'm still trying to calculate how to pay him back.

Dinner and golf are too much for a make-up date.

Jax pushes open the door and waves me through ignoring the tiny yellow pencils and paper to keep score. "We'll skip keeping score this time so you can get the hang of it," he says when he sees where I'm looking.

My eyes roll of their own accord once I've stepped out into the warm night air. I can never tell Spence or my brothers about this. There's no way they would ever let me live it down especially since I'm considering throwing the game.

All in the name of love.

Jax throws an arm over my shoulders which seems to be his favorite thing to do tonight and tugs me to his side as we walk to the first hole. My wavering smile drops right from my face the second I see the two people waiting to play. Jax's arm slips from my shoulder when I immediately step away.

You have got to be kidding me.

19

Spencer

Zoe slips a hand into my back pocket and tugs me against her not caring that we are at a family establishment with a group of five little kids on hole one. Four feet away.

"Children present," I say as I grip her wrist and force her to let go without being too aggressive. The action only spurs her on though, and a giggle escapes her right as her lips find the hollow of my throat. A tongue follows as her fingers tuck inside the waistband of my jeans.

PDA isn't my thing and I'm definitely not for it when we are getting dirty looks from parents.

I turn my face away as she leans up on her tippy toes aiming for my mouth and my heart plummets through my feet and into the ground most likely on its way to the Earth's core when I see the two people standing behind us.

Freaking A.

I wiggle out of Zoe's grasp and smile through the clench in my jaw.

Rylee's gaze bounces between Zoe and me several times before flicking off to the side. "Hey, Spence."

"Rylee, uh, what are you doing here?" I scratch the back of my neck where I can feel prickling from Zoe's burning glare. After all, I shut her down the second Rylee showed up. An ego hit that big has got to hurt.

"Date, remember?" She twists the club between her hands without so much as glance my way.

"Right. Right. So you decided to burn off some calories from dinner?"

Invisible fists with the strength of Mike Tyson pummel my stomach to a bloody pulp when Jax wraps his bulky gorilla arms around her from behind. "Well, Rylee here is about as good at mini golf as she is at riding that cute little board of hers. Figured she could use some pointers."

My snort draws three sets of eyes. One of which is burning with irritation. Whether from my reaction or Jax's outlandish comments, I'm not sure. Yet it doesn't stop me from throwing out my next words. "So great you came along to help her out. Maybe you can give her some pointers on riding that *cute* little board too."

This time I know her irritation is directed at me when she flips me off the second Jax's back is turned. She opens her mouth seconds from ripping into me judging from her sour expression when Zoe jumps forward.

"Hey! Let's play together. Couple versus couple."

Smart. She drew a line in the sand quick by marking us as a couple. Not a box I would check, but I don't argue.

"No thanks," Rylee and I blurt out at the same time Jax grins and says, "Sure."

The way Rylee's wide eyes meet his and the quick puckering of her lips tells me I'm in for a whole night of torture. If she's letting him talk about her boarding skills, there's no way she will stand up to him over a game of golf. A game she could whip his butt in on her worst day. Not to mention the aching desire to break every single one of his fingers whenever he touches her. Would love to see him catch a football after that.

I turn away, not able to look at her anymore as her shoulders drop and she nods. I understand she likes the douche, but this is so far beyond ridiculous. Nothing like my Rylee and I can't stand the sight of whoever this imposter is.

"We're up." Zoe links her arm through mine and tugs me toward the first hole where the family is collecting their balls. "Who wants to go first?"

"Ladies." Jax waves her forward earning a grin from Zoe and a tight smile from Rylee. "Don't worry," he mock-whispers to Rylee. "I'll show you how to swing when you get up there."

Jesus. This guy...

Zoe steps forward and hits her green ball hard enough to almost launch it into the second course. She giggles and slaps a palm to her head as it ricochets around before coming to rest close to where it started. "Guess I'm not very good at this."

"It's all in the way you grip the putter." Jax steps up behind Rylee as she drops her ball on the blue runway. "All about the hands." Jax positions his hands over hers, wrapping his arms around her in the process and pressing his body to hers in a way that makes my blood freaking boil.

It takes everything in me to stay still and not throw him over the ledge into the water.

Jax remains at Rylee's back and swings with her, hitting the golf ball way too hard and sending it past the hole. The first hole. The easiest one on the whole course. A shot Rylee has hit on the first try multiple times.

She shrugs as if responding to my thoughts and slides away, her eyes meeting mine over Jax's shoulder. "Guess it takes a while to get the hang of it."

"No worries. We have eighteen holes." Jax winks and takes his shot—again with too much force—and ends up about where Rylee's ball is.

With it being my turn I know for a fact I could sink a hole in one no problem and show this gorilla how it's *really* done. But when I see the scowl on Rylee's face I change my mind. Winning him over is what she wants. And I'm sure she's loving every second of his hands-on lesson even if she could whoop his lame ass all the way to next Sunday.

My ball rolls to a stop right next to the rest. Okay, slightly in front of the rest.

Zoe lands the shot in the next swing and does a little shimmy that under normal circumstances I would find cute. But I'm too distracted by Jax's hands all over Rylee as he once again sets up her grip all wrong. The girl is tall, no way she should grip it that low.

She misses and lets out a growl of frustration. I'll be surprised if this act continues for another seventeen holes. She's the most competitive person I've ever met. One time she flipped the Monopoly board when she was on the verge of losing to Noah. We were fifteen and on Christmas break. Ended the merriment really quick.

"Don't worry, you'll get there." Jax unleashes a smile that even has Zoe tripping all over herself as he hits his ball in. "It's that easy." He holds his arms out to the side with all the ego of a small-minded guy.

"If it's that easy shouldn't you have gotten it on the

first try?" I ask as I hit the ball in. Two seconds later I'm on my ass with Rylee standing above me glaring.

Did she actually shove me? And for what? To defend the baboon.

"Oops." She extends a hand, a breathy laugh covering her malicious intentions. "Tripped. Sorry."

Oh, it's so on.

I dust my jeans off, ignoring the smirk Jax is throwing my way. I'm sure he considers my fall karmic retribution or whatever, but I have to play nice now for my plan to succeed.

"You know, this will get boring after a few holes." I slide an arm around Zoe, planting a kiss on her temple. "Why don't we make it more interesting?"

Jax's eyebrow jumps up. "How?"

Yeah. He's just as competitive as she is. Has to be to play football.

"A little wager. The losing team has to jump into the school pool Monday morning wearing all their clothes, then finish the day. Without changing." My gaze cuts to Rylee who is struggling to rein in her anger.

It's a bet we came up with at the beginning of the year. One we were saving for the last day before summer break for whoever had the most wins at mini golf.

I smile, focusing on Jax who is fidgeting with the putter. He doesn't seem to be the type of person who likes to lose. Which is why it will be oh so much fun to whoop his ass.

"I second that idea," Zoe says, as she bumps me with her hip. "The only thing that would make it better is if you were topless."

"You're assuming we're going to lose." I wink, which does the trick and gains a giggle.

Rylee's left eye twitches, and she glances away but not before her carefully constructed persona cracks and fire lights her eyes.

"I'm game." Jax switches his attention to Rylee. "You up for the challenge?"

"Sure. Why not?" Her face is so pinched with restrained anger her head might explode at any minute.

Oh, she's so going to kick my ass when she gets me alone.

We move to the third hole—a windmill thing with a steep ramp. The family in front of us has moved on two more holes giving us some space. We'll need it because the second Rylee starts losing, the faint grasp she has on her temper is going to snap. With that comes a lot of swearing.

"Watch how it's done." Zoe swings her hips as she walks to the red-and-blue carpet.

Her confidence is high for how she's been playing, but the stink-eye her words pull from Rylee when she overheard sure makes up for her lack of skill. As expected, Rylee can't help but succumb to the competitive drive. It's the reason we never took boarding too seriously because it would ruin it.

Zoe misses by a long shot, her ball rolling up the ramp, then back toward us, leaving her right where she started.

Rylee's glare turns calculating as she stomps her way to where I'm standing. Hole three is where our battle of who is better at mini golf started. Well, it started with a lucky shot from her and then spiraled into monthly games with her brothers that eventually became just the two of us.

I'm the only guy who can handle the wildfire running through her veins. Even her own brothers are no match. Can't hang when the inevitable ass-kicking comes around followed by cocky trash-talking.

She knows it too, that's why she's putting on this ridiculous show for Jax. And I'm hoping her wild side is too strong to stamp down.

Rylee swings, moving her hands to the proper position for her height and sends the ball rolling on a perfect line for a hole in one. When it sinks, I can't help but smile. For the briefest of moments, she grins back, reveling in her win. But the second Jax wraps his arms around her stomach the smile drops, replace by phony shock.

"Wow!" Her hands come to rest on his forearms and I back away, running an agitated hand through my hair. "Guess you are a great teacher."

"That was freaking amazing, babe." He plants a kiss on her cheek causing Zoe to swoon beside me and throw in an annoying *aww*.

"Your turn, Lever," I snap, crushing the moment like a bug on a windshield.

He shoots me a funny look as he steps away from Rylee who is currently wishing for my death. Every ounce of irritation reserved for her brothers is directed at me.

"You okay?" Zoe asks from my side, her hand trailing up and down my back.

"I'm fine. We're just holding people up." I thumb over my shoulder praying there are people there because I sure didn't check before spouting off the lame excuse.

"Oh. Whoops." Zoe cringes, confirming my reasoning, and waves to the people behind us. "Almost done. Sorry!"

After I sink my shot in the first try, winning another glare from Rylee and a very handsy hug from Zoe, we move on.

The next few holes pass with little conversation. I can tell Rylee is concentrating on reining in her anger when Zoe sinks a hole in one and she misses. Although I think she missed on purpose. Two quick lessons don't make you a pro and would seem odd even to a guy with raw hamburger for brains if she sank every hole on the first try.

By the eighteenth hole, I'm certain Zoe and I will win. Any other time I wouldn't be as confident because Rylee is a freak who can make this shot blindfolded. We tried one time. In fact, that was the last time her brothers played with us. But this new Rylee might throw the game to win over Jax.

Not that she would need to. He hasn't been able to keep his hands off her all night. Because of that, my putter might have a slight bend in it that wasn't there before. Took everything in me not to bash him upside the head with it when he pressed his lips to her neck after a lucky shot on hole ten.

"You're up."

I blink and shake my head and Zoe shoots me an odd look.

"Sorry." I glance at her empty hand, then to Jax and Rylee because if I zoned out that hard I missed them all taking their shots I have other things to worry about.

Jax stands empty-handed but Rylee tilts her head to the side when I notice she still clutches her ball.

"Don't I go last?" I ask.

Zoe leans against the black railing, crossing her ankles. The movement forces her skirt up a few inches giving me a glimpse of toned thighs. Guess I should have noticed earlier. Why else would she wear that knowing we were going to play mini golf? Her grin has me clearing my throat as I turn to Rylee.

Rylee tosses the golf ball in the air and catches it, raising an eyebrow. The challenge is clear. "Why don't you show me how it's done?"

She knows I'm the worst at this hole. It's the reason she's beat me so many times. With our scores being so close, all it would take is another *lucky* shot from her to come out victorious.

And for me to end up fully clothed in the school's swimming pool.

Not to mention another one of Jax's smug looks.

I shake out my arms as I step up to the red carpet. Rylee's gaze follows me the whole time, no doubt judging every move I make. Normally, she's more vocal about it but Rylee 2.0 can't make it public knowledge how good she is at, well, anything she puts her mind to.

The orange ball hits the carpet with a soft thud that sounds way louder than it should. As my arms shift back, preparing to launch the ball as hard as I can, Rylee clears her throat and I stumble forward missing the ball.

"Thought." Her hip pops out as she leans into Jax. There's no mistaking the devious glint in her eyes. "What if we up the ante? Say...the losers have to jump into the pool during swim practice."

My mouth drops open and Zoe squeals behind me.

"But, Mr. North is like the meanest teacher at Roseville," she whines. "We would get detention for the rest of the year."

"Then you better hope Spencer makes his shot." Rylee smiles, but it's not warm. Shit, it's not even friendly. "What do you say, Hendricks?" Her hardened gaze lands on me and I know without a doubt she will make this shot.

And now I can't back out. Even if it was just the two of us. Rylee would never let me live it down.

"Deal." I extend my hand expecting her to take it, but she glances away, leaning her head on Jax's shoulder.

Fine.

With a deep breath, I line up my shot again. Nerves have my palms sweating so much the rubber on the end of the putter is doing little to keep my grip solid. There's no way in hell I want to draw the wrath of Mr. North, but it seems now I have little choice. Even if his ideal punishment will be making us clean the pool or worse yet, make school pride banners for their meets. Yeah, I've heard he's done that in the past with kids he deemed troublemakers.

At the last second my hand slips and I hit the ball on the edge sending it sideways instead of straight up the ramp. When it reaches the end, it launches the other way and lands...right in the water.

Rylee's roaring laughter almost forces me to dive into the shallow water to retrieve the damn ball and go again, but seconds later her ball hits home causing the bell above to sound. Not only did she win a free round next time—because no one makes this shot—but she also won the bet.

And Jax's heart, apparently.

He scoops her into his arms and spins her around with a triumphant shout. When he sets her down, her face is flushed and she stumbles to the side.

"That was such a lucky shot, babe!" Jax grabs her face and leans in but she steps back and runs her fingers through her hair.

"Crazy, right?" Her gaze skips over me, instead focusing on Zoe. "So, I guess we win. Yay. No wrath from Mr. North. But that also means..." She grins at Zoe who is pouting by my side.

"Wait, you were serious? Come on. Mr. North is crazy. I could get kicked off the cheer squad for that."

"Oh, come on, princess. I'll put in a good word for you." Jax tugs Zoe to his side and together they walk to the entrance.

Rylee stays behind, eyes trained on me.

"Really?" I ask, leaning on the putter.

"What?"

"You know what."

"Hey." Her hands fly up in the air. "You started it. But maybe you should get boarding out of your system tomorrow." She walks away throwing parting words over her shoulder. "You won't have time with detention."

20
Rylee

The sun feels amazing as I lay out on one of our blue-and-white deck chairs. We may not have a pool, but it's never stopped my family from soaking in the sun's rays whenever possible. Although the second summer hits, really hits I mean, I might be tempted to beg my dad for a pool yet again. Even one of those tacky aboveground kinds will do.

Can't always rely on Spencer. Especially with the way he's been acting.

I push my sunglasses back up my sweaty nose for the tenth time in the past hour. What I should be doing right now is boarding with Spence. But after he left in a hurry last night, I haven't heard from him. His car didn't show up in his driveway until after two in the morning.

Okay, yes, I couldn't sleep and it might have something to do with the fact that he left with Zoe suctioned to his body like some bloodsucking pest hell-bent on burrowing deep and never letting go.

I still don't know why the sight of them together bothers me so much. But my already awkward date took a steeper nosedive when they showed up. Pretending to be someone I'm not with Jax alone was hard enough. Add Spencer to the mix and my anxiety shot through the roof.

That's got to be what bothered me so much. It wasn't Spencer with Zoe, but that they crashed my date and

Spence took every opportunity to undermine my behavior.

And I took the bait.

I couldn't help it. His stupid taunting and disappointed glances were enough to make me break. I made the shot I've made every single time we've played for the past few years. Of course, I played it off as if Jax was the best teacher on the planet. In reality, he sucks.

With a groan, I toss my arm over my eyes. I shouldn't have pushed the bet further. No way in hell did I want to watch from the sidelines as Spencer completed *our* bet with Zoe. And I certainly didn't want to lose my ride home for the rest of the year when he's saddled with detention.

With Zoe.

But he got under my skin and I couldn't let it go.

My phone rings and I jump at the sound of "Thunder" filling the silence.

Spencer's ringtone.

"What?" I snap the second I pick up.

"So, a good night's sleep hasn't bettered your mood?"

"I wouldn't be in a bad mood if you hadn't crashed my date."

Spencer's gasp almost makes me smile. *Almost.* I can picture his stupid face twisted in mock horror. "I would never crash. I can't help it if we're on the same wavelength."

"Sorry, buddy, you were on Jax's wavelength last night. Mini golf was never in my plan."

The line goes dead for a few seconds before Spencer clears his throat. "Take a day off from your double life and hang out with me? You were supposed to dedicate yesterday to me. Instead, lover-boy got all your attention."

I roll over on the lounge chair, my body suddenly a bit too hot despite being early morning. "And why should I grace you with my presence after how you acted yesterday?"

"Because this might be the last time you see me. Rumor has it, the last kid who messed with Mr. North's pool disappeared."

"Yes, and aliens exist too."

"Just come over, Everett. I might be nice and let you swim in my pool."

This gets my attention and I shoot up. "Really? It's never up and running this early in the year."

"Yeah, well, Dad wanted to get a head start." There's a weird twinge in his voice. Almost sad, but he brushes it off with another sigh. "You coming or what?"

"I should be icing you out after how you acted."

"Will snacks and music of your choice make up for it?"

I stand and slip my feet into my sandals. Thankfully, I had thrown on my new swimsuit this morning with plans to roast in the sun for a bit and get used to it. Jax expects to see me in one and I can't be a fidgeting mess. "I suppose." I try to lace my voice with annoyance but fail. "Be there in two seconds."

Spencer starts to count down as I hang up on him. Mom and Dad left to go do something this morning and my brothers are out being stupid, so I race through the side gate and jog across the street.

Both of Spencer's parents' cars are gone. Again. I swear they are never home. No wonder he was spending so much time at my house. Well, until the whole Jax thing happened. Now he spends as much time with that skank Zoe.

Ugh. I rake fingers through my hair in annoyance at the mere thought of her being here. Her car is nowhere to be found so I think I'm in the clear. *Better* be in the clear.

We need today. Will be good for us. For our friendship. I might even get him to tell me why he's been acting so weird. It's got to be his parents' divorce. Hell, I didn't see that one coming.

Spencer opens the door with a grin. "Took forty-six seconds."

I reward his sass with a soft punch to the gut. The drama king folds over groaning. "Baby." I shove past him, goosebumps trailing over my exposed legs when the cool air inside his house hits me. "Do we need to make a snack run?"

"Nah." He shuts the door, tilting his head toward the kitchen. "Mom went shopping yesterday."

"Dr. Pepper?"

"Of course."

"Then we're set for now." He trails after me as I make my way to the kitchen. There are a few brown packing boxes lining the hall. They must be doing some spring cleaning.

"So, what's your issue?" I ask as I grab the six-pack of bottles from the fridge.

Spencer's friendly smile dims. "What are you talking about?"

"You've been pissy ever since Jax and I started hanging out. Scared you're going to lose your best friend?"

He scratches the back of his neck, refusing to meet my gaze. "Nah. Just think he's a dick and not worth your time. But, uh, anyway, let's go swim."

He shoulders past me, sliding out the door before I can respond. I knew he didn't *like* Jax. I didn't know he thought he was such a bad guy. For crying out loud, he was the one who agreed to help me land him.

And then quickly bailed...

Spencer is in the pool when I step outside onto the cement patio. I catch sight of his glistening shoulders before he dives under the water. Which gives me an idea.

"Hey!" I shout when he surfaces by the diving board. He whips toward me, pushing the hair off his forehead. "Let's play underwater secrets."

His loud laugh is genuine and infectious. "Haven't played that in forever."

"All the reason to play now." I kick off my sandals as I tug my shirt over my head.

Spencer's eyes go wide and it takes me a second to realize why and what he's looking at. Butterflies erupt in my belly as my hand flies to my bare stomach. For a second there I forgot I had it on. When I bought new clothes, I decided to brave a real bathing suit. Although this one could pass for scraps of fabric. The tiny black triangles cover all the important bits but still leave me feeling naked.

The bottoms are worse because of my bubble butt as my mom calls it.

"Does this look okay?" My fingers hover over the zipper of my shorts. Spencer nods but says nothing. "You think, um, Jax will like it? He mentioned a trip to Lake Tahoe."

He glances away brushing a few drops of water off his shoulder. "Yeah. Sure. He'll love it."

His words don't match the anger in his voice and I'm positive I killed the mood again. After a few seconds of hesitation where I'm certain he'll kick me out, I slip off my shorts and they join my shirt on one of the lounge chairs.

The hot cement burns my feet as I race toward the stairs in the shallow end. Normally, I would cannonball in as my grand entrance, but I'm not sure how this suit will hold up.

The cold water feels incredible as I sink down to my chest. Spencer floats against the wall on the other side, hanging on to the lip and still not looking at me.

"I'm glad you invited me over."

A snort is his only response. It says everything he's *not* saying. Right now, he's wishing he never called me. All this feels so damn weird. Never in all the time we have known each other has there ever been silence when we are together. Not even during a movie.

My nervous, awkward, overwhelming energy makes me blurt out the first thing that pops into my head.

"So you and Zoe serious?" I cringe and sink lower into the water hoping he didn't hear me. If he says yes, it might tempt me to drown myself.

Speaking of people who aren't worth the time. Spencer is nothing but a passing fling to her. The thought of them becoming official sends heat flaring through my chest.

"We're just hanging out," Spencer answers as he pushes off the wall. "She graduates this year and I—" He shakes his head. "No reason to get serious."

"Oh. Okay." Relief floods through me and I wade farther into the pool until my feet no longer touch the bottom.

"What about you and Romeo? He confess his undying love for you yet so you can cut the act?"

I scoff and float toward him. "No. Just hanging out too. He's kind of hard to read."

Spencer mumbles something under his breath, creating tiny bubbles on the surface of the water.

"What was that?" I ask.

"I said we should play our game."

"Sure. Sure." My hand hits the surface of the water sending a small tidal wave right into his face. "I'll go first."

Before he can get me back, I sink under the water. Soon after Spencer follows, swimming close enough that we can see each other's faces.

"You're a terrible liar!" I shout, but it comes out all muffled and creates enough bubbles that I lose sight of him for a second.

When he comes back into focus he waves a hand, signaling for me to say it again. With the last bit of oxygen I have left, I repeat myself then swim to the surface.

Man, I have got to work on that this summer. Spencer never outlasted me underwater before.

Next to me, Spencer sucks in a gasp of air and once again pushes the hair off his forehead. "I got you are." Water hits me in the face and I gasp, floating away from him. "You can't tell a secret about me."

"Sure I can." I clear my vision and smile.

"Clearly against the rules. But we'll count that as a practice round. What was the rest?"

"I said you're a terrible liar."

His laughter rumbles, somehow hitting me right in the stomach and shaking my insides. "That's not a secret."

I shrug and kick my legs to stay above water. "Your turn."

With a shake of his head, he comes closer. "No way. You didn't even tell a real secret."

"Fine," I relent. He'll never let it go and the whole point of today is to get our friendship back on track. Suppose I can throw him a bone. I sink under the water and let a truth bomb out. "I'm scared I'm losing myself."

It's something that's been bothering me since the party. Festering. Every time I throw on one of my new outfits, and parade around I feel a sadness that grips my heart. At first, the excitement of Jax noticing me overshadowed it. But it became crystal clear last night when I went along with his golfing lessons. It seems like such a small thing, but I didn't even fight it. Just went right along with it, giggling and acting how I'm sure every other girl he dates acts.

No wonder Spencer couldn't look at me most of the time. I was pretty disgusted with myself when I got home.

Both of us break the water at the same time.

"You okay?" His hand slides across my cheek, knocking a chunk of hair out of my eye.

"Yeah."

His eyes soften as he moves closer. "You'll only lose yourself if you forget who you really are underneath all these fancy new clothes. Don't get yourself twisted over some guy."

I smile despite the sadness weighing me down. "You were always too good at this game."

"Nah. Just dialed in to the Rylee channel."

My hands slip around his neck, linking as he treads water. "That's gotta be rough."

"Most days." He grins when I dig my heel into his thigh.

"Tell me truthfully, should I stop this?"

"Jax?" Spencer kicks a few times sending us to the center of the pool.

"Yeah."

"Of course you should. You're too good for him." His eyes search my face before his sighs. "You're too good for all the moron guys at our school."

"What about you?"

His head jerks back, mouth dropping open. "What about me?"

"Zoe."

His shock morphs into confusion. "What's Zoe got to do with anything?"

I roll my eyes. "Come on. She's not your type."

"My type, huh? And how do you know my type?"

"Well, for starters, blondes aren't your thing. You normally go for brunettes. Big brown eyes. Tall..." Spencer's arms tighten around my back, fingers playing with the ends of my long brown hair.

Wait...did I just describe myself?

His eyes hold fear and I swear his breathing kicked up a notch. In response my stomach flips, making my breathing race to catch up to his.

"Rylee, I—"

"You two are getting in some swimming while you

can?" Spencer and I both whip our heads toward the voice.

Mrs. Hendricks stands at the end of the pool, a wide brim hat covering most of her face, but I do catch a sad smile.

Spencer lets go and drifts toward the deep end. "It's warm, figured we would waste the day here instead of the skate park."

"Wise choice." Her fingers fiddle with the charm around her neck. "God, so many memories of you two out here." Her heavy sigh deflates her shoulders as her chin trembles. "It's going to be hard to let that go." With those parting words, she rushes inside, shutting the sliding door behind her with a rattling bang.

"What does she mean let it go?"

Spencer stretches an arm across the cement ledge. "We graduate next year."

"Right. Which is a little early to be so emotional, isn't it?"

"You know moms." Spencer lifts himself out of the water, giving me a great view of his muscular back. "I should go check if she needs help with lunch. Then I, uh, have a date with Zoe." His gaze meets mine for a brief second before tugging on his shirt. "So, I guess I'll see you tomorrow?"

Did he just dismiss me?

I climb out of the pool as he dries his hair with a towel. Before I reach my clothes, he's inside the house. With numb legs, I step into my shorts, then throw my shirt on not even caring they will be soaked by the time I make it across the street.

My stomach hasn't stopped quivering and it's starting

to freak me out. What he said... The way he looked at me... In all the years we have been friends I have never felt that way.

The way I *want* to feel when Jax looks at me.

I bolt from the backyard using the side exit so I don't have to go through the house. As my feet slap on the hot concrete all I can do is pray whatever this is passes before I see him tomorrow.

I can't be falling for my best friend. It will ruin everything.

21
Spencer

Stupid. Stupid. Stupid.

It was all I could think about as I lay awake all night staring at the boxes lining the floor. Empty boxes because I hadn't started packing because I'm still hoping my parents will call off the divorce.

About as stupid a thought as telling Rylee how I feel.

Which is what I almost did.

I almost ruined everything. Our friendship. Life as I know it. Because if I had told her I would have to follow it up with me moving and destroying our plans for the future.

But God, I wanted to tell her. It wasn't the plan when I invited her over but then she brought up Jax and I couldn't lie. And then the bikini. God, that bikini.

I never knew a girl could look that good in a bathing suit.

With burning eyes, I prop my hip against the driver's side door of my car. This morning Rylee never showed up for a ride to school. Ten minutes before we were supposed to be in class, I knocked on her door only to have her mother answer and tell me Rylee was feeling under the weather and would be staying home.

Under the weather my ass.

That's when I realized how bad I'd screwed up. Even though I didn't get the chance to spill my guts thanks to my mom's impeccable timing, Rylee still picked up on it.

Same wavelength.

So now I'm standing in my driveway holding a pint of her favorite ice cream, an offering I bring every time she is sick. Only I can't convince my legs to work to walk across the street and knock.

Her parents are still at work so at least that would save me some embarrassment when she stabs me in the heart and tells me the only feelings she has are ones of friendship.

Her eyes said it all. Dread. She was just as relieved as me when my mother broke us up.

My phone chimes in my pocket and despite my terrible mood, I answer it.

"Hey sexy," Zoe purrs.

I turn away from Rylee's house and rest my elbow on the roof. "Hey." There's no excitement in my voice but that doesn't seem to faze her.

"So, I was thinking instead of sitting here all alone that you can come keep me company. Netflix and chilling alone is sad."

If that isn't an invitation to hook up I don't know what is.

I twist around in time to see Ryan pull up in his beat-up Mustang. "Yeah. Sure. Give me twenty minutes?"

"Can't wait."

I end the call and jog across the street before Ryan gets to the porch. He nods in greeting and hikes his book bag over his shoulder.

"Sup?"

"Hey, man." We stop short of the front steps and I kick

a loose piece of dirt on the edge of the grass. "I was wondering if you could give this to Ry for me?" I hold out the pint of ice cream but he just stares, making no attempt to take it.

"Why don't you bring it in?"

"Oh, I uh, don't want to risk getting sick."

This makes his eyebrows jump because never in all the time we've been friends have I cared or avoided Rylee when she was sick. In fact, most of the time I would be right by her side watching terrible movies until she felt well enough to get out of bed.

We even ended up at the hospital together when we were twelve and a mean case of strep throat sent our fevers sky-high.

"Oh...kay." Ryan takes the carton from me but doesn't leave.

"So. Thanks." I turn, but his next words stop me.

"She's not really sick."

Without facing him I ask, "Oh, yeah?"

"I've faked enough illnesses to spot one when I see it. Her cough was over the top."

"Well, I'm glad she's doing good. Take the ice cream if you want it." I take two steps toward the sidewalk before Ryan's hand on my shoulder stops me.

"Look, I'm not about the whole mushy moment thing, but I meant what I said the other night, tell her."

This time I spin to face him. An eerie calm has taken over my voice. If only it would spread to the rest of my body so I could slow the frantic beating of my heart. "Tell her what?"

"I heard your mom talking to my mom. If she knew

you were moving in a couple of weeks, I think she might feel differently about this whole Jax thing."

My laugh comes out a little manic. "Please. She's finally got what she wanted. She's not giving that up because I'm moving."

Ryan nods once and glances toward the house. "Maybe she doesn't realize she has options."

My heart skips a beat knocking the wind out of me. There's no way. *No way* Ryan knows for sure. I've been too careful when her brothers are around, too afraid they might kick the crap out of me for simply thinking of her like that. But the sympathetic expression on his face says otherwise.

"Give her a chance. She might surprise you." He punches me on the shoulder and turns for the house.

Or crush me.

"What's the point?" I ask as he opens the front door. "Won't change the fact that I'm moving."

Ryan grins and shuts the door before responding or giving me a chance to ask what the hell that look was for.

My phone chimes in my pocket again, this time a text. A glance at my watch tells me I'm already late getting to Zoe's.

Not that I'm in the mood now. But since my best friend couldn't even be bothered to tell me she was faking an illness, or come down to talk to me, I climb into my car and back out of the driveway. A bit too aggressively, but whatever.

As I'm turning down the road, I glance at Rylee's window right as the drapes fall.

So, she is avoiding me. Well, if that's how she feels then I will make myself less available.

22
Rylee

The sound of Ryan's and Spencer's voices drag me out of bed and to my bedroom window. One that overlooks the driveway where both boys are standing. Spencer holds out a pint of ice cream and my heart flips up into my throat.

Word of me being sick must have gotten to him. Well, pretending to be sick, but he doesn't know that part.

And now I feel like a total jerk.

Yesterday freaked me out so bad I couldn't sleep. Not a single second. I lay awake running the moment in the pool through my head over and over in an infinite loop. Each time it got worse. The tension in my muscles grew. My heart wouldn't stop skipping.

The crappiest part is I couldn't talk to the one person I would normally go to with a problem.

So, when morning came, and I looked like freaking death it was easy to convince my mom I had come down with something.

I should have told Spencer, but again, how could I without explaining my reasoning? He could see through my fake sickness in two seconds flat and I would be left waffling, trying to come up with an excuse he would believe.

Which is why I stay hidden in my room and watch him talk with Ryan. What I really want to do is crack my window so I can hear what the hell they're talking about, but that might give me away.

And lord knows how I will act because my feelings are still so twisted.

Every single time I think about how right his hands felt on my back and how close our faces were, butterflies throw a party in my stomach. It leaves me more confused and spiraling into self-doubt.

I can't tell Spencer this. He will laugh. Call me crazy. Tell me it's never going to happen.

Then he'll end our friendship.

Not worth it. Whatever this is will pass. I just need to refocus on Jax. My hormones are a little confused. That's all.

Spencer reverses out of his driveway, squealing to a stop before glancing my way. In a moment of panic, I let the drapes fall into place and step away praying he didn't see me spying on him. Because, hello, that is out of character for me and screams, *hi I'm hiding from you!*

I flop on my bed and ten seconds later Ryan bursts through the door and throws the container of ice cream at me. Thank goodness for my fast reflexes. I catch it before it can smack me in the face and sit up scowling.

"What do you want?"

"Your boyfriend left that for you."

I choke on air then scramble to cover up my reaction and stomp down the swell of fluttering in my stomach. "Spencer isn't my boyfriend."

Ryan leans against the door smirking. "Right. And I'm Iron Man."

"What are you babbling about?" I prop the container on my knee.

"Oh, I thought we were telling lies."

"Get out."

"Ha! I knew it!" He takes two steps into the room and shoves his pointer finger in my face.

"Knew what?" I grab it and twist, causing him to hiss and jerk away. "I coulda told you Mom and Dad were planning on converting the basement into an apartment because they figure you'll spend the next four years repeating the twelfth grade."

"You only deflect when I'm on to your feelings." Ryan waves his fingers at me in a weird jazz-hands move.

"Or when you're annoying me by simply breathing." I grab the ice cream and shove past him. I don't want it to melt all over my bed and the thought of eating it alone is so sad I want to cry.

Ryan follows me down the stairs, his heavy footfalls making me wish I was an only child.

"You should tell him how hard you're crushing."

I whirl around on the bottom step. Ryan doesn't have enough time to stop and slams into me, knocking me back and onto my butt. The ice cream goes flying and since it's half-melted when the lid pops off, it splatters the floor and wall in mint green liquid.

"Oh, look what you did, you idiot!" I jump up and race over to pick up the carton before more leaks out.

"What I did?" Ryan's hand smacks against his chest and I swear he almost looks sincerely shocked.

"Can you go away?"

"Hey, I'm trying to help my baby sister out."

"I'm younger by three minutes," I mumble as I set the container down on the island and grab a wad of paper towels.

Ryan stands in the doorway not making a move to help clean up the mess *he* caused.

"Isn't there some other girl you can annoy with your personality?" I ask.

"Nah. I'm free tonight."

"Lucky me." I shove his chest and slide through the tiny opening it created. The poor white runner is saturated. No way I'll be able to clean this up and hide it from Mom.

"Back to what I was saying," Ryan grumbles from behind me.

"That for once you would leave me alone?"

"No." He tosses a whole roll of paper towels at me when we both realize the small amount I'd grabbed won't make a dent in the mess. "Tell Spencer how you feel."

"I don't even know what you're talking about." Ice cream soaks through the paper towels, making my hands all sticky and adding to my annoyance. Ryan hit way too close to home. I hate that he can pick up on my feelings so easily.

Stupid twin ESP or whatever.

"Come on. I would rather Spencer be hanging around than Captain Butthole."

"Are you talking about Jax?" I say, standing up, taking all the used paper towels with me. There's a noticeable stain on the rug but will do for now. I'll blame it on Ryan later.

"Of course I am."

"What is everyone's issue with Jax?"

Ryan follows me into the kitchen. "He's an asshole."

"You don't even know him."

He laughs and shakes his head. "Are you that naive? Guys talk and let me tell you, Jax Lever talks."

This catches my attention and I spin around, glare armed and ready. "What are you implying?"

His hands fly up in the air. "Hey, bro code and all that. I'm just saying you should dump the moron and be honest with Spencer."

This right here is why I avoid conversations with my brother. "Did you seriously say the words *bro code* to me? Because if you did, pretty much anything that follows is null and void."

Ryan blocks my way as I try to leave him and this ridiculous conversation behind. There's nothing to tell Spencer because whatever I'm feeling is a fluke. A confused firing of my hormones.

"Move." My fist hits his stomach hard enough to make him grunt, but he remains planted in the doorway.

"Listen, my nice brother routine has reached its end—"

"Good."

"But, I'm just saying I would prefer to *not* beat Lever's ass."

"That's exactly what Will said."

"Because the dude sucks."

"Duly noted." This time Ryan moves when I shove him and I race toward the stairs hoping if I put a door between us he'll leave me the hell alone.

"Just talk to Spencer," Ryan calls after me. "He'll be easier to beat up if he hurts you."

I slam the door hard enough to shake the pictures on the wall. What is up with my brothers being so anti-Jax.

Will hangs out with the guy from time to time and until now, Ryan wouldn't care if I dated a farm animal.

Because I'm in a self-punishing mood, I find myself at the window staring down into Spencer's driveway where his car is still missing. He's probably over at Zoe's. Hanging out. Or making out.

A sharp pain bounces through my stomach.

Well, good for him. If he's happy, I'm happy.

That's what I tell myself as I climb into bed. A bonus of skipping school and not getting dressed is that I'm ready for bed at a moment's notice. And that's all I need. After a solid night's sleep, I will wake up and realize I had an off day.

I don't like Spencer. Not like that.

I nod once to myself as I turn off the light. But even as I talk myself into a more rational thought process, I can't get the fluttering in my stomach to stop.

I'll have to beat up Ryan tomorrow for putting thoughts into my head. Then I'll ride to school with Spencer and everything will be how it was a couple of weeks ago.

23

Rylee

Spencer didn't respond to my text this morning telling him I'm going to school but he is waiting in his driveway for me with a giant smile on his face.

"It lives."

"Barely," I lie as I slide into the passenger seat.

"You didn't miss much yesterday. A big test in history. Ryan got slapped by Vivian Greywood in the cafeteria. Oh, and worm aliens took over the entire student body, but I single-handedly saved everyone."

"Funny." I flip down the visor mirror and make sure the eyeliner I put on is still in place.

"Okay, you caught me. But Vivian did slap Ryan. Apparently, she was under the impression that they were exclusive."

"She's dumber than she looks."

I smile and flip up the visor. See. Completely normal. Spencer hasn't mentioned Sunday because there is nothing to talk about. I should never be alone with my thoughts. It's dangerous.

Spencer flicks his blinker on but turns left when he should turn right for the school.

"Mind if we make a pit stop?" he asks when he catches my questioning glance.

He's the driver, so it's not as if I have much say in the

matter, but I wave him on. Three minutes later I wish I had put up a fight.

Zoe bounds down the brick steps to her house, and waves at Spencer who couldn't look happier if he tried.

As if he won the freaking lottery or something.

Zoe stops by his window and leans in to give Spencer a wet kiss on the mouth. In response, my stomach almost loses its hold on breakfast.

"Oh, hey, Rylee. Didn't know you would be joining us."

Us?

Us?

It takes everything in me not to scream. Has this girl lost her mind? She's been in his life all of five seconds and she thinks there is an "us"?

"Um, babe, I hate to ask but I kinda get car sick. Is there any way I can ride with you up front?"

My mouth drops open. Seriously, I think I feel my chin brush against the lace lining the lower half of my camisole.

Spencer turns to me, a grimace distorting his face. "Do you mind?"

Do I mind? Of course I mind. "No problem." I crawl through the space between seats instead of getting out because I'm not so sure what I'll do if I come face-to-face with Zoe.

She slides into *my* spot and plants another kiss on Spencer's mouth.

Oh, yup, Peanut Butter O's don't taste as good on the way back up.

"I had so much fun last night," Zoe coos and tugs his hand over to her lap.

I knew he was with her.

The scenery flies by as Spencer drives us to school. I've never looked forward to arriving but that circle of hell certainly beats the one I'm in now.

I can barely breathe with how much perfume the girl is wearing. And her voice. Dear lord, how does Spencer listen to that all the time? Nails on a freaking chalkboard.

"I can't believe they killed off Freya," Zoe says and rips me right out of my thoughts.

"Wait." I lean forward, forcing my head between the puppy eyes she is throwing his way. "Did she say Freya dies? As in Freya Swan from *Dead Walking*? You better not say you watched the season four finale without me."

Spencer winces, releasing a hiss that confirms that yes, he did, in fact, watch *our* show with some random chick.

"Wow." I sink back into my seat.

This is one of the worst friend offenses he's ever done. Major violation. It's up there with forgetting birthdays. No, you know what, it's worse, because he didn't have the decency to ask me first.

I hop out of the car the second he's parked.

"Ry, wait." His words follow me as I march toward the front door but he sure as hell doesn't. Nope. He's standing by his car with that...leech wrapped around him.

I throw the middle finger over my shoulder waving it high and proud to make sure he sees it.

And to think I wasted my sick day yesterday.

———

By the time lunch rolls around I'm still as angry as I was

walking into school. In fact, my mood took a steep nose-dive when I caught Jax walking with Haylee. Not abnormal or anything. They do all run in the same circle. But the fact that he ignored me kind of stung.

I stab my spork into a tater tot and drown it in ketchup. The second I pop it into my mouth, a shadow falls over the table.

Spencer meets my glare head-on although I do catch a slight flinch when I first meet his gaze.

"What do you want?" I ask and add another tot. Hopefully, I'll choke on them and fall, hitting my head giving me amnesia so I can forget this morning.

His red tray hits the table across from me as his long legs step over the bench seat. "Still mad then?"

"Oh, no. I'm super stoked that you cheated on me by watching our show with some chick. It's every best friend's dream." I take a swig of my soda, letting my gaze drift over to where Jax is sitting. With Haylee. Awesome.

Today can't get any worse.

"Listen, I'm sorry. She asked me over and had it on."

"Cool. So, when I invite Jax over and we start season five, you'll be completely fine with it?" Spencer shrugs, which sends my anger over the edge. "Maybe I'll take him to the park and show him how to grind. I have that extra board in my garage. It was going to be your birthday present but it should go to someone who I'm assuming has better skill."

Spencer's lips pull into a tight line. "What the hell is your problem? It's just a stupid show."

My problem is that he ditched me to watch it with someone else. He couldn't even be bothered to bring my ice cream up when he thought I was sick. Too concerned with sucking face and stabbing me in the back.

"Not like you've been around," he grumbles and takes a bite of his sandwich.

My mouth pops open, then snaps shut. Crap. He's right.

"Okay." I run a hand over my cheek, trying to calm down. "Okay, you're right. I've been a little MIA lately. I wasn't even here yesterday to make sure you ended up on Mr. North's shit list, though I heard you bitched out." My lips tip up into a half smile, but Spencer's don't. "Truce?"

Truth be told, my reaction might have been extreme. Yes, watching our show without me is considered cheating. Normally when he annoys me, I punch him and move on. So, what the hell *is* my problem?

Another tray falls to the table with a loud clatter, drawing my attention away from my best friend's surprised face. Blue eyes shine as Zoe throws me a huge smile and wraps Spencer in an almost possessive hug.

Anything I was about to say dies. Actually, more than my words die because when she twists his head to the side so she can plant a sloppy kiss on his lips, something cracks in my chest. A gaping, ripping sensation that leaves me gasping for air.

I stand, jerking back so quickly I almost trip over my seat. "I gotta go."

Spencer stands, shrugging Zoe off. "Ry—"

"No, I uh, have to grab notes for English from when I was sick. No big deal." I pick up my bag from the floor, trying to avoid both Zoe's and Spencer's gazes, only to land on Cora one table over who is watching us with rapt attention as if this is some daytime soap.

Great. I'll hear about this tomorrow.

On my way out of the door, while I'm paying zero attention to what's in front of me, I run smack-dab into a wall of muscle clad in a black polo.

My gaze jerks up and right into gorgeous blue eyes. I let out a shaky laugh as Jax rights me, keeping a hand on my shoulder. Right then is when my stupid traitorous brain directs my attention behind me where I see Spencer scowling at me. He doesn't even seem to notice Zoe who is trying desperately to get his attention.

"Rylee?"

My eyes snap back to Jax. "What?"

There's a second of irritation on his face before he laughs it off, and pats my upper back. "Falling into my arms rattled you that hard, huh?"

His friends laugh, ones I didn't notice were standing on either side of him until now. One of them elbows Jax in the side and he throws me a cocky grin before continuing on.

"I asked what you are doing tonight?"

"Tonight?"

"Yeah, like after today." The irritation grows on his face. He must not be used to girls who don't give him their full attention.

"Oh, sorry, my mom is dragging me to some charity event."

Not a total lie. She asked me this weekend to which I replied "hell no." But hanging out with her and a bunch of women as they sell baked goods to raise money for a new roof for the church suddenly sounds a hell of a lot better than hanging out with Jax.

He steps closer to me, trailing a hand up my arm. "Too bad, because my parents are out of town."

His two friends snicker behind him. Did he just imply I would come over for sex?

"Rats." I snap my fingers then cringe. Did I just say rats?

Jax's face falls as he takes a step away from me, running fingers through his hair. "Oh...kay then. Guess I'll see you tomorrow?"

"Yup." I sidestep him and rush down the hall to the course of his friend's laughter.

I have a strong feeling that is the last time Jax Lever ever tries talking to me.

When I arrive home, the last thing I want to do is talk to my parents. Yet, they both stand on the porch speaking in what appears to be calm words.

This will last only so long...

I drag my backpack with me as I climb out and cast a worried glance across the street at Rylee's empty house before turning my attention back to my parents. I guess this is what I deserve for not coming right home and locking myself in my room. It's not as if skating helped my mood. The place was crowded as all hell and every time I hit an impressive trick, I wanted to rub it in Rylee's face. Only she wasn't there.

She was probably off with her boyfriend celebrating the fact that he couldn't keep his hands off her while half the school watched.

He made his pursuit of her public knowledge. By tomorrow everyone will know.

Yippee.

"Hey, Spence." I scowl at my father who smiles.

I swear he loves pissing me off.

"What are you doing here?" The irritation in my voice is clear making my mother frown.

"Your *father*," my mom bites back, making it clear I need to shape up, "is here so we can sit down and talk about this whole moving thing."

"Joy." I shoulder my bag and walk past them. "Seems kind of pointless though."

My mom is the first one to follow me in, sending me a warning glance. "I think you'll be pleased with the decision we both came to."

"Can't wait to hear what new plan you've come up with to ruin my life." I slump on the couch as my dad sits in the recliner in front of me, all humor from earlier gone from his face.

I should feel bad, but now he has a taste of what he's put my mom and me through these past few months.

"Spencer Jacob Hendricks," my mother admonishes as she sits next to me. "Knock off the attitude right now."

I press my lips together until they ache. Now that I've dished out a slice of the resentment simmering inside, it's kind of hard to stop.

"As you know, your father and I put the house up for sale," she continues when she's sure I won't butt in. "However, after talking I decided I can wait to move home until you've graduated. Your father will be buying a small place out in Sacramento and I'll be renting an apartment nearby so you can finish at the same high school."

My heart races faster with each word. There's no way my father did something selfless. I don't even think he knows that word anymore.

"Did you hear me?" my mom asks.

I nod, not sure what I should say. Thank you maybe? But we never should have come to this point. They should have been thinking about how their actions would affect me from day one, not scrambling at the last second after being called out.

"Someone is already interested in the house," my dad says, eyes flicking to me for a brief second. "Which means we will be in a rush to get the house packed."

"Okay." I nod, knowing I have at least ten empty boxes up in my room. Ones that sat there as a symbol of my defiance when it came to the move.

"By this weekend," he finishes.

My stomach drops out of my body. This weekend? Man, they really don't give a crap about how I feel about this whole thing. Yes, I'm no longer being dragged across several states, but still. Four days to say goodbye to the only house I've known since I was a kid. Not nearly enough time.

I sit in stunned silence. Really. This has got to be the longest any of us sat together in a room and not shouted. Mom keeps shooting Dad worried glances until he clears his throat and stands.

"Which means you should start packing. Now."

Right. I nod and stand, giving my mom a small smile as I pass her. It's been a long time since they have been civil and even though I don't agree with their decision, I'm not going to mess with the tightrope of civility they are walking.

Although I do expect some kind of blowout while I'm upstairs because, let's face it, my dad can't keep it together that long.

My bedroom door clicks shut behind me and I stop, resting my head on the cool wood as I survey the room I grew up in. Behind my headboard is a hole from Ryan's foot after a board game went south and Rylee couldn't handle the loss. She had pushed him a good five feet. Spitfire of an eleven-year-old. The window has a crack in it from a rogue football. It's when I learned I'm not too good at those kinds of sports and wouldn't be following in the elder Everett brothers' footsteps. And somewhere there's a stain on the carpet from an out-of-hand paint war when we were eight.

I grab a handful of stuff off the oak bookshelf by the window and drop it into a nearby box. The next armful knocks loose a green-and-orange friendship bracelet Rylee made for me at camp when she was ten. That was a long summer what with her not being right across the street. Six whole weeks of boredom. It was the summer Ryan and I became sort of friends. But he wasn't Rylee and no one ever would be.

She's going to flip when she finds out I'm moving. No longer a hop, skip, and a jump away.

A flash of light catches my eye and I peer out of the window just as Rylee hops out of her mom's car wearing a long white dress. Even from here I can tell she's annoyed, but she gives her mom a tight smile and makes her way to the front door.

That's when it hits me like a freaking bolt of lightning thrown by Zeus himself.

I'm not leaving.

My hand tightens on the friendship bracelet that's torn and frayed from the time it spent around my wrist. Two years to be exact before it was too gone to last another day.

I'm not moving to Washington.

Which means....

My heart pauses before jumping up into my throat to beat wildly. I don't have to do this anymore. I only agreed to help Rylee land that moron because I thought I wouldn't be around to make sure she was happy. But now...

I stumble back from the window. I can fix this. She listens to me. My stomach drops again and I'm so not up for this gastric roller coaster. But my gut knows something my stupid heart is refusing to listen to. And that's the fact that Rylee *used* to listen to me. Past tense. Ever since Jax started showing her attention, it was as if she became obsessed with it. Possessed is more like it.

But that doesn't mean I can't try. I *have* to try. Starting tomorrow.

I can do this. I can get us back on track and maybe...I swallow down the hope fighting its way to the surface. We will never happen, but the least I can do is make sure she's not wasting any more of her time with that idiot.

I nod once to solidify my thoughts and sweep more junk into a box. That will have to do for tonight because right now I have to text my best friend and tell her she's all mine tomorrow.

25

Rylee

"You're in a good mood this afternoon," my mom calls from the kitchen.

I grin as I toss my backpack down by the pile of shoes. I am. I really am. Today has been a breath of fresh air and I feel more like myself than I have in weeks.

Spencer was waiting for me this morning with his usual smile on his face. When I asked if we were stopping to pick up Zoe because she had to be what put that smile there, he shook his head and opened my door. Shotgun. Right where I belong.

The day fell back into place. Zoe didn't join us at lunch although I saw her shoot a few nasty looks his way, which meant their time ran out but not on her terms. Something I'm sure she's not used to.

Jax never tried to talk to me and Haylee seemed too pleased with herself as she hung all over him at their table. After my behavior, I expected as much. The weirdest part though was how little it bothered me. Not even a pang of jealousy.

And now, I'm going to change so Spencer and I can hit the skate park for some much-needed boarding. Nothing, and I mean nothing could kill my vibe right now.

My mom clears her throat as I grab my board out of

the coat closet next to the door. "And where do you think you're going, young lady?"

"Um, to the park?"

"Nuh-uh. Tonight is the church fund-raiser. Will and Ryan already canceled dates so you might as well call Spencer and tell him you'll have to go another time."

Ah. There it is. I forgot about my mom's innate ability to ruin anything fun.

"Mom—"

"Nope." She holds up a hand, silencing me. "You're going. End of story. So, march your butt upstairs and change into something presentable. I laid an outfit out on your bed."

By something presentable, she means something girly. Which after everything shouldn't bother me, but it does. She's commanding me to do something as if I'm some child who can't dress or think for herself. I've never regretted giving her an inch more than this moment.

And whoever heard of a stupid two-part fund-raiser. I spent all last night parading around as perfect daughter Rylee. Lasted all of two hours. Needless to say, she was peeved when I disappeared to hang out with the little kids. Slides and monkey bars aren't the best thing for a white dress, but anything was better than faking a smile that could rival Miss America.

"So this is another one of our *perfect* family moments?" I ask, tossing the board back into the closet hard enough to leave a dent in the wall.

"Go upstairs," she commands, the vein in the middle of her forehead popping out.

"And if I refuse?"

"Then you can kiss freedom goodbye until graduation."

"I'll be eighteen in a few months. Then what?" I cross my arms over my chest, well aware of how childish I sound. But for crying out loud she already dragged me to some tea party last night with a bunch of women I haven't seen since I was five. That, of course, came with dressing me up like a doll.

"Rylee N—"

"Noel Everett," I finish for her. "Yeah. Yeah." I wave away the rest of her rant. The last thing I want is to spend the night filled with suffocating tension. So I have to wear another dress. Not as if I was so against the idea when I thought it would win over Jax. When it *did* win over Jax.

I stomp upstairs to the sound of her banging around in the kitchen. Will is glowering at me when I reach the top.

"What?" I snap, shoving him aside so I can maneuver into my room and shut the door.

"You really had to piss her off? Now she's going to be on everyone's case."

"I aim to please."

Will rolls his eyes, leaning against the wall with one foot resting on the doorframe, blocking my escape. "Would it kill you to be nice to her for once?"

"Probably." I elbow his stomach, trying to limbo underneath him, but he doesn't budge.

"Did you ever stop to think she doesn't know how to relate to you?"

This gets my attention and I stop trying to shove past my wall of a brother. "Huh?"

"Think about it, genius. She has three boys and a girl who wishes she was a boy." I stick my tongue out not even gaining a smile. Or scowl for that matter. Just a flat almost bored expression. "Dad's got sports with you and guy talk with us. What does Mom have?" His foot hits the floor with a loud thud, making me jump. "You were willing to change who you were for a boy. Maybe you can stop being so stubborn for a second and at least *try* with Mom."

I stand frozen with my mouth hanging open as he saunters down the hall to his room. Seconds before the door closes, I regain my composure.

"Since when did you become the levelheaded one?" I ask. Out of all of us, he used to be the one whose temper could be compared to a raging forest fire. Yet here he is counseling me as if he never smashed a controller against the wall when he lost in some stupid video game.

"Since I realized I leave in a few months and all Mom will have is you and Ryan. Sad future," he says through the crack then closes the door.

Okay. So perhaps he's right. Something I will never admit to his face because his head is about five times bigger than Spencer's and I don't need to inflate it more. But still. I suppose it won't kill me to put a little effort in with my mom. There is only one year left before I'm living several states over.

I twist my mouth to the side as I consider my next move. It would be nice to have peace in the house this summer. Would also be nice to get my mom off my back and maybe, just maybe, get a bit more freedom. It's not as if I hate all the girly dresses. In fact, I quite enjoyed the attention I got from Jax when wearing them. I guess it comes down to how much I hate being told what to do.

The door clicks behind me and I come up short when I notice the outfit laid out on my comforter. There's not a hint of floral in sight. No ruffles. Nothing pink. Instead, a simple purple-and-black plaid shirt dress is resting next to my black leather jacket. And on the floor sit my black Vans.

My fingers shake as I run the fabric through them. This outfit is so me. Something I would pick out for myself. The perfect mix of girly and tomboy. Can't skate wearing it, but I don't mind rocking it out in public.

Dang. She *is* good at this.

I pull the dress on, pairing it with black leggings to cover the bruise still healing on my knee. It's gone all yellow, which somehow looks worse than the deep purple of last week. Once it's on, I'm in awe of how good it looks. Of how good I feel.

My mom hit it out of the park.

"Hey, Ma!" I call from the upstairs hallway. Five seconds later she comes into view, a deep frown still making her forehead. "You think you could help me with my hair?"

Dear lord.

Her eyes mist over and I swear she looks as if I told her Santa was real. And that I do believe in fairies. Sprinkle some unicorn glitter in there too and none of that would match the expression on her face.

"Y-yes of course." She climbs the stairs in a flash and pulls me in for a tight hug, almost cutting off my air supply. When she leans back her eyes are no longer on the verge of spilling over but she's got a giddy smile going on. "The way you wore it on your date the other night looked great, but how about we try a messy ponytail?"

A smile stretches across my face matching hers as she nudges me toward my room.

So this is what common ground feels like.

"You staying for the game?" Wills asks as he sets dishes in the sink.

We were left on our own tonight. Mr. and Mrs. Everett had tickets so some show and so they told us to order a pizza and try not to make a mess of the house.

Trust at its fullest because I swear I saw a devious glint in Ryan's eye. Thankfully, Will crushed whatever he was thinking with a promise to keep us in line. A promise he would do anything to keep. He's turned into such a suck-up.

I hand over the remaining plates and try to keep my gaze off Rylee, which is hard considering the low-cut tank top she's wearing.

"I have homework I should probably get to."

"But the game is about to start," Ryan says from behind me.

"If he's staying, it's to hang out with me and not you losers." Rylee saddles up next to me bumping my thigh with her hip.

We've been back to normal these past few days, which has been nice. Better than nice. Which is the exact reason I chickened out on talking to her about the move and Jax and everything. I did, however, talk to Zoe and told her we couldn't continue with our relationship. If it can even be called that. Judging from how her mouth was plastered to Micky Donaldson at lunch, she took the news well.

Rumor has it—and by that, I mean overhearing her friend talk about it during PE—she's been after him for a while but he wouldn't give her the time of day. Until she was with me. Funny how that works.

Guess our hookup was mutual in terms of convenience.

"Better leave your bedroom door open," Will mutters as he places the last of the plates into the dishwasher.

"Shut up." Rylee shoves past him on her way to the refrigerator. "That rule only applies to guys I'm dating. This is Spencer we're talking about."

I meet Ryan's gaze over her head and he cocks an eyebrow. There's that glint of mischief in his eyes again.

Rylee tosses me a soda that I almost don't catch, too busy trying to decipher what's going on in Ryan's messed-up head.

"What do you say, Hendricks? Wanna stay and watch Will cry when the Sharks lose?"

"They're not losing." Will slams the dishwasher shut and stomps out of the room to our laughter.

"Sure."

Rylee links her arm through mine and tugs me toward the living room. "He's always so testy on game nights. Plus, from what I overheard this afternoon, Ellie broke up with him for the hundredth time. Wanna take a bet on how long it will be until they're back together again?"

"By the end of the week," Ryan says as he elbows Rylee in the back sending her to the side and right into my arms.

Whoa. My heart shoots up into my throat as her hands land on my chest, fingers digging in as she regains her balance. Ryan snickers as I grip her hips and steady her, my thumb grazing against bare skin where her shirt rode up. And just like that my hands let go as if she's on fire and I'm seconds away from being burned.

"Asshole," Rylee yells then whips her attention to me. "He's been unbearable this week. Tell me again how we're related, let alone womb-mates?"

I nod, but no words form on my tongue. I'm still very aware of the fact that we're standing in the doorway so close together I could lean down and plant a kiss on her full lips with little effort. She also hasn't tried to take a step backward and I swear I felt the ghost of her fingertips over one of my pecs before her hands fall to her sides.

Rylee's cheeks tinge pink, resembling how they look after an afternoon in the sun. Fear takes over because I swear I'm thinking loud enough for her to hear. In the next breath, she steps away leaving my arms feeling empty.

"So, how many comments do you think it will take to make Will lose his cool? My guess is four considering his team is up against mine." She winks and turns away, jogging into the living room.

Was I reading too much into that? I swear there was a hint of longing in her eyes. Or maybe I'm muddling my own emotions. No wonder she got out of there as soon as possible. If I keep this up, she'll be running for the damn hills.

When I get to the living room, Will is sitting in his

dad's recliner, absorbed in the game. Two minutes in and we've already lost him.

I step toward the couch, but Ryan props a foot up, stretching to where he's taking up the whole thing.

"Move, idiot," Rylee calls from the two-seater on the other side of the coffee table.

"Nah." Ryan yawns and stretches his arms over the side of the armrest before shooting me a wink.

You've got to be kidding me. Is he seriously doing this on purpose because he thinks I like his sister? Okay, so I do, but I never came out and admitted it. And if he doesn't cool it she'll catch on. The last thing I need is for her to jump to conclusions or hear secondhand information before I've gotten the chance to tell her how I feel. About Jax that is. Because I'm never telling her I love her.

Whoa—!

I swallow so hard my throat aches. The *L* word bounces around in my head making it ache. Do I love her? Is that what this terrible aching feeling is every time I see her with Jax? Every time I *think* about her with Jax.

Ryan clears his throat and I realize I've been standing there spacing like a weirdo for God knows how long.

Letting out a groan, I plop down next to her, my thigh bumping into hers and sending a bolt of electricity through my chest.

I should have gone home.

"You okay?" Rylee whispers and tucks her feet under to give me more room.

No. No, I'm not. Now I'm acutely aware of the way my heart skips at the slightest of touches. How my body gravitates toward her with a need to touch any part of her if only for a moment.

This is so not good.

"Mmm-hmm," I grunt and press my hip into the armrest trying to give myself even an inch more of space.

"We could—"

"Game!" Will shouts and gestures toward the TV where the puck was stolen by the other team.

Rylee rolls her eyes and leans her head on my shoulder in a totally normal move she's done at least a thousand times. Except now all I can smell is her shampoo and my heart won't calm the hell down.

Damn Ryan. Why did he have to push? Why is it he couldn't drop it so I could focus on something else. Anything else. But I know now this won't ever be something I can shove into the corner of my head and forget about. My heart won't let me. Now that I realize the truth of the matter, Rylee and I will never just be friends again. My stupid heart can't take it.

So now I have no freaking clue what I'll do because Rylee and me, we're never going to happen. Not the way I want us to.

With a sigh, I rest my head on hers and focus on the game. Might as well suck in these moments while I can. Because I'll have to tell her. Whether it's today or a year from now, I'll have to tell my best friend that I'm crazy in love with her, then stand there as she rips my heart out of my chest and hands it back to me.

"Shit!" Will turns off the TV and throws the remote, filling the quiet room with a loud bang as it hits the wall and the batteries spring out flying everywhere.

His team lost, which means he'll be absolutely delightful for the rest of the night. This always happens, and is the exact reason I try to avoid watching games with him. Zen Will may make an appearance when it has to do with our parents, but sports? Not a chance.

"Next time, bro." Ryan pats the armrest and sits up grinning as Will runs an aggravated hand through his short hair. He's never looked so much like our father until this moment. "So what are we going to do with the rest of the night?"

The clock on the wall confirms it's close to ten. My curfew extends to the time people need to leave the house. Even Spencer. My mom's generosity and leeway depend on her mood. And now we have a shattered remote to explain.

"I should probably go," Spencer mumbles and rubs both palms into his eyes. He's been so quiet the whole night I jump at the sound of his voice. Had I not seen his eyes open watching the game I would have thought he was asleep.

"Boo." Ryan chucks a pillow at his face, almost hitting me in the process. I glare as Spencer tucks the pillow under his arm. "It's Friday night and too late to go anywhere now. Please don't tell me we're all going to file upstairs to go to bed."

"That's exactly what we're going to do." Will stands, stretching out his back with a grunt. "After you take out the trash."

"Do you believe this?" Ryan thumbs at Will, his face morphing into one of disgust. "A few chest hairs and he thinks he's Dad."

Now it's my turn to cringe away, gagging at the image of my brother's chest. "TMI."

"It's not the chest hairs that make the man it's the bal—"

"Ew! Okay!" I jump up, cutting Will off before he can finish that sentence. "I don't need nightmares."

"Seriously." Ryan shoves my head, knocking me back on the couch with a palm to the face. "What are we doing?"

Growling, I push him away, narrowing a glare at Spencer when all he does is laugh. Traitor. "You're going to take the trash out like Stand-in Dad said and I'm going to walk Spencer to the door. I don't want to get grounded. Not when we have a whole Saturday planned at the skate park." I bump Spencer with my shoulder who nods in return.

A whole Saturday uninterrupted. It's been forever.

"You heard your sister," Will says in perhaps one of his worst ever impressions of our dad.

"Come on." Ryan throws himself on the love seat, landing on my lap with his stinky feet in my face.

"Get off." I shove but that only gets me an elbow to

the thigh. "Spence, a little help?" He's sitting next to me, avoiding Ryan's long limbs all while laughing.

When he shrugs, I reach over and wrap an arm around the back of his neck in a tight headlock and tug him toward me so he has to suffer through what is the smell of death coming off my twin's feet. We can't be related let alone part of the same DNA.

"Idea!" Ryan rolls off me, doing a backflip to land on the floor at my feet. I use the opportunity to give him a shove, sending him tumbling over the coffee table.

The fake plant and coasters go everywhere when he reaches out to stop himself. Nothing works though and he ends up stomach-down on the white carpet.

"Guys!" Will bellows and reaches down to help him up. "I refuse to be responsible for an ER visit. Save it for when Mom and Dad are here."

"Yeah, Ryan. Gotta be more careful."

He levels me with a glare and straightens his shirt. "As I was saying... y'all won't leave and I refuse to go to bed at —" he glances at the clock "—nine forty-seven on a Friday. So what we really need is a game of hide-and-seek in the dark."

Will snorts and heads toward the kitchen. Spencer and I both look at each other and roll our eyes.

When we were kids, it was our favorite game. Used to drive the babysitters nuts. But that was because we were fantastic hiders when we wanted to be and one time, a sitter actually called our parents in a total freak-out when she thought we had snuck out. None of us were over the age of eleven with Ryan, Spencer, and me around seven, so I'm not sure where she got that bright idea from. Our dad found us all crammed in their closet. Somewhere along the way we stopped trying to find each other and found it far more entertaining to mess with the babysitter.

It was the last time she sat for our parents and hide-and-seek was officially banned from the house. At least when the 'rents were around.

"We're way too old for that game," I say as I stand.

"We're never too old to have fun."

Out of the corner of my eye, I catch Spencer nod in agreement. "You can't seriously want to play." He shrugs at my words, which gains a mischievous grin from Ryan.

"You're not still afraid of the dark are you, Riles?" There's that stupid pet name again. Ryan sounded way too much like Jax when he said it that I've got to think he's been around school spying on me.

"Of course I'm not."

"You sure you're not still scared one of your dolls will come to life and hunt you down?" Spencer hides a smile behind his fist when Ryan elbows him.

"I hate you," I throw at Spencer as I make my way to the kitchen.

Truth be told, I took way longer than most kids to no longer fear the dark. Until I was about twelve to be exact. A topic my brothers loved to throw in my face whenever I would run down the hall to the bathroom. Or be caught in the same hiding spot as Spencer because he would never leave me alone knowing I would freak out. He was always there, grabbing my hand and telling me it was okay even when we shimmied under the bed and I thought we were about to be sucked into some monster realm.

"So we're doing this." Ryan trails me into the kitchen, turning off every light on his way.

"Have fun with that." Will drops a detergent tab into the dishwasher, then turns it on.

"Oh, no, big bro. All or nothing." Ryan jumps up into the island, grabbing a grape from the fruit bowl. "This might be your last opportunity to hang with us like this."

Those words get his attention and I see the exact moment he gives. Stupid Ryan and his ability to talk anyone into anything.

"Fine. One game." He holds up a pointer finger as emphasis.

This won't last one game.

It never does.

"Ugh. Fine!" I throw my hands up in defeat. "But no outside. Or the attic. Everywhere else is free game."

"Anything else, Your Highness?" Ryan asks.

"Yes...not it!" I touch my nose as fast as I can and grin as Will and Spencer follow suit.

Ryan groans and slumps forward on the counter. "Lame."

"You know the rules," I singsong as my hand latches on to Spencer's. He stiffens at the contact but after a few seconds, his fingers tighten on mine.

And the butterflies in my gut go wild. To them, it's as if they are front row to the Super Bowl instead of the run-of-the-mill friendly handholding going on.

"Yeah. I know the rules." Ryan walks over to the corner and thumps his forehead on the wall. "You got one hundred seconds. Make em' count."

Will, Spencer, and I glance at each other as he yells

"*one*" loud and clear. Then hell breaks loose as we all shove our way out of the kitchen at the same time.

We might put up a fight, but the truth is we all love this game. We played it over summer break last year when Noah was home visiting and my parents took an overnight trip out of town. It was the night Ryan got locked in the attic and we had to add it to our no-go list.

I yank Spencer up the stairs, muffling a giggle when he trips and catches himself on the top step.

"Try hiding *alone*," Will calls from the hallway.

Yeah right.

I hold a finger to my lips as I lead Spencer to Ryan's room. I haven't stepped foot in here for years. Too afraid of what I might find. Which is what makes it the perfect hiding spot. He'll never think to go here first.

We maneuver around the crap littering almost every inch of the floor until we reach his closet.

"He's going to kill us," Spencer whispers.

I shrug and crack open the door, sliding inside and shutting it the second Spencer follows.

If I thought his room was bad, this is so much worse. I have no idea how he fits all this crap in here or why, but the ground doesn't even feel even.

I stumble forward when my foot catches on something and smack right into Spencer's firm chest. His hands come up, gripping my hips to steady me.

"Sorry," I mumble, but I can't stop my fingers from tracing the prominent online of his pecs just like they did earlier. And just like earlier, I can't help the squeeze of my gut when I remember how good he looked topless in the pool. All wet and muscular and tan. Pretty sure I had it all wrong. Jax isn't the Greek god I've made him out to be, Spencer is.

An unintentional gasp escapes me because, hello, this is my best friend I'm having dirty thoughts about, and my face rushes with heat.

"You okay?" he asks.

It's so dark I can only make out the outline of his body, but I've stared at his face so many times over the past nine, almost ten, years, I can imagine exactly how it looks. Eyebrows scrunched in. Lips pulled down at the corners. He's concerned because he thinks I'm having some freak-out about being locked in the dark.

Not that I'm wishing I could trace the outlines of his muscles without clothing in the way. Because if he knew that, he would run out of this closet faster than I could blink.

"Yeah." I clear my throat, making sure there's no sign of the breathlessness I feel. "Just wondering how Ryan will exact his revenge when he finds out I was in his room."

"In some very imaginative way, I'm sure." His voice sounds strained. Almost husky.

"That's what I'm scared of." My hands drop to Spencer's arms. Only then do I realize he's still holding on to me.

When my legs step forward without permission of my brain his grip tightens, digging into the soft curve of my waist. His breath ghosts against my lips, coming in quick pants that match the sudden thumping of my heart. We've been closer than this before. Hell, we've slept in the same bed so why—

His lips crash into mine. It happens so fast my

thoughts screech to a halt and I have no time to prepare myself for the way my stomach twists or the stabbing sensation through my heart.

Heat rushed through my limbs, bringing with it a flood of emotions I can't quite decipher. After several thunderous heartbeats, the shock melts away and I kiss him back. My lips mold to his, holding on for dear life and trying to keep up with the frantic mingling of breath and hands as he takes control of my mouth and obliterates any grasp I have on rational thoughts.

And then he's gone.

In a lightning-fast move, Spencer lets go and slams into the wall behind him, knocking a box off the top shelf with a noise loud enough to alert Ryan of our hiding spot.

Spencer exhales and all I can do is stand there and wonder if I just hallucinated. There's no way my best friend just kissed the stuffing out of me and set fire to a burning need in my veins.

"Rylee, I—" I shut him up with a kiss.

Yup. Apparently, that's what we're doing now. It's wrong. I shouldn't be doing it and yet I can't tone down the need to touch him. To kiss him. Now it's as necessary as breathing and I can't deny the urge.

Spencer stills under my touch. The firm muscles of his shoulders tense under my hands. For several agonizing seconds, I think he might deny me. I'm back to wondering if I had some lucid fantasy. But then after one ragged exhale, his arms wrap around me bringing me flush against his body.

And then there's nothing but sensation.

Our location slips away.

Time no longer matters.

The anticipation of being caught somehow makes this so much more frightening yet electrifying.

Spencer kisses me in a way I never knew possible. His tongue slips inside my mouth, gentle but demanding, and I'm gone. So gone. I never knew I could want a person like this before. Desperation is the only thing that comes to mind. I'm desperate for his touch. Desperate for this to never stop because I'm afraid my heart might shatter into a thousand pieces. I may not be able to go another day and not experience this.

Spencer pushes me backward until my spine bumps into the wall. The weight of his body on top of mine is extraordinary. Safe. Warm. Loved...

The realization hits me at the exact moment the closet door flies open.

"Gotcha!" Ryan yells, and I jump slamming my head into the clothing rod.

I groan, rubbing what I'm sure will be a lump and pray he didn't see us. But he did. I know it because for the first time in his entire life, Ryan has gone silent. Mute. And so, so still.

Being the coward that I am, I run, leaving Spencer alone to deal with my brother and with no explanation from me. I can't. Not tonight. Not before I have time to think about what the hell just happened.

But even as my door clicks shut behind me, I know. The way I've been feeling the past few weeks becomes blatantly clear.

My fingers drift up to trace my still tingling, swollen lips and I know.

I've gone and fallen in love with my best friend.

And now nothing will ever be the same.

28

Rylee

Mere hours after closing my eyes I wake up and the familiar pang of fear is back. It might be early afternoon, but I won't be able to sleep away the truth.

I kissed my best friend last night.

No, correction, I made out with my best friend. Hard. And daylight hasn't brought any clarity to the matter because I still want to do it again, every day for the rest of my life. Even at the risk of our friendship.

That exact thought stops me from getting out of bed and running across the street. Nothing should be more important than our friendship.

Sure, he kissed me first, and he didn't hold back, but it doesn't mean he feels the same way I do. It doesn't mean...

I groan and bury my head under all my pillows praying for some weird disease to come along that causes short-term amnesia. There's no way in hell I'll ever be able to move past what happened last night. If I see him, I'll want to be in his arms with his lips all over me. If I see him with another girl, I'll want to punch her face off caveman-style and claim him as mine.

Might as well call this the black plague of our friendship because that kiss, that mind-numbing, amazing, confusing, extraordinary kiss, ended my life as I know it.

"Hey, loser," Ryan calls from the doorway.

"Go away," I mumble from under my pillow fort. But I know he heard because his laugh rumbles through the quiet room.

"So, you and—"

"Go away!" I shout, sitting up and knocking the pillows on the floor. I am so not having this conversation with my infuriating other half. All he'll do is mock me.

But when I sneak a peek at his face, there is no mirth there. Just a slight smile and understanding in his eyes.

"What do you want?" I ask.

He shrugs. "Wondering if you wanted breakfast. Mom made waffles before she had to head somewhere. Not sure where because I stopped listening."

I stare at him for a few seconds. Is he letting me off the hook? No way. Ryan would never let an opportunity to torture me slip by. He probably alerted the whole house and they are waiting downstairs to mock me mercilessly.

"I'm not hungry."

"There's fresh strawberries."

I glare. He's not luring me out of this room with food.

"Fine," he sighs. "You also have a visitor. I shoulda' mentioned that first. He's on the porch."

Fear strikes my gut so fast I almost puke. Early this morning I texted Spencer that my mom sprang some girly trip on me and I wouldn't make the skate park.

Did he see my mom leave without me?

Crap.

I bolt from the bed, pulling my hair in the messiest ponytail known to mankind and rush down the stairs. All my previous reasoning flew right out the window because knowing Spencer is here, right downstairs, jump-started something in me and the need to be near him can no longer be ignored. I guess my limit of self-control is walls and an entire street separating us.

The front door bangs against the wall drowning out Ryan's laughter as I rush outside. And run straight into a wall of muscle. Except this isn't the chest that pressed into mine last night.

Horror slides through me in a wave turning my legs into Jell-O when I glance up and am met with sparkling blue eyes and an amused smirk.

Jax.

Jax is here on my porch.

And I'm dressed...my gaze flicks to my sweatpants and an oversize shirt. Awesome. I resemble a hobo. Not that it should matter how he sees me. Yet I can't stop embarrassment from heating my cheeks.

"Well, aren't you adorable in the morning." He smiles, flashing me his perfect teeth. "Or I should say afternoon."

"I had a late night." My hands slide over the side of my head, trying and failing to smooth down flyaways. Nothing but a shower and strong hair spray will get rid of them at this point. "What, uh, what are you doing here?"

His large body leans toward me and I fight the urge to lean away. "I was in the neighborhood and thought I would see if you were free for lunch."

"Oh." Yeah, that's all I have because after my freak-out at school we haven't spoken. Not once.

"Or." His eyebrow quirks and his jaw ticks. "You can come with me to Malcolm's party tonight?"

"Another one?" Oh, kill me. My brain needs to regain control of my mouth pronto.

"Yeah. Another one." His warm hand cups my cheek

as he takes another step forward, boxing me in against the wall. "And maybe this time you can stay for the whole thing."

Apprehension must be clear on my face because he laughs, filling my nose with the sweet smell of alcohol. Is he already drinking?

"Don't worry." His lips hit my earlobe sending goosebumps down my arm and freezing me in place. "It's at his house this time. No need to pee behind a tree."

The next second his lips are on mine in a sloppy kiss. My fingers flex on his shoulders, keeping him from coming any closer as my brain has a freaking meltdown, leaving me frozen from shock.

It lasts only a few seconds before he puts a few inches between our mouths, a dopey expression on his face. "Incentive," he whispers, then pulls away.

I fight the urge to run inside the house and scrub the sensation of his hands and mouth off of me in the shower. Instead, I force a smile. "Um. I can't make it tonight. And I don't think you and I...are going to happen."

Anger flares on his face, setting his jaw and jutting it forward. From this angle, he kind of resembles a baboon. Just like Spencer said.

Spencer.

Shit.

My gaze flies over Jax's shoulder, and sure enough, my best friend is standing on his porch with murder in his eyes.

"Thanks for the invite though." I pat his chest as he takes a stiff step backward. This might be the only time in history he's been flat-out turned down.

Without another word, he turns from me and thumps down the front steps. I wait until he's pulled away from the curb before risking another glance at Spencer, but he's gone. His front door is wide open but he's nowhere.

Shoeless and with little thought, I run across the street and up his front steps, bursting through the door, panting.

Spencer isn't there, but boxes litter the floor. Everywhere. It looks nothing like the house I've been in thousands of times.

This is more than spring cleaning.

"Spence?" I call. Furniture is all wrapped in plastic. No pictures are on the walls. Panic hits me full force as I stumble up the stairs. "Spence?"

I find him in his room, staring out the window with hands clenched into fists. He's mad. I get that. Jax kissed me hours after he did. This can't look good, but if he'll let me explain he'll see I don't want to kiss Jax. The only lips I want are his.

"Get. Out." Spencer growls in a voice that sounds nothing like my best friend.

"Spence, I—"

"Get out!" He roars, turning on me with such hatred in his eyes I can't even breathe let alone move. "Are you deaf? I said get out of my room. My house. My life!"

Ragged breath enters my lungs as my chin trembles. This is what I was afraid of. Of ruining our friendship. And now the situation is so much worse because of Jax.

"Spence, why—"

"You know what, it's fine." He shoulders past me, stomping down the stairs as I follow him with absolutely no words forming. "This isn't my house for much longer. You stay. Invite your boyfriend over."

I watch his tense back round into the kitchen as all life drains from my limbs. Did he just say this wouldn't be his house much longer? Yes, he said other things, absurd things, but that's all I can focus on.

"Where are you going?" I wheeze out as I stand in the hallway watching as he wraps glasses in bubble wrap.

"To Washington."

Nope. I was wrong. There goes the last bit of life in me along with stupid, stupid hope. So that's what the kiss had been about. He knew he was leaving. He knew he would never have to face repercussions. Why not kiss his best friend? Who cares if I fell for him when he'll never have to deal with it?

Tears form on my lower lashes but I refuse to let them fall. Knowledge is power and he'll never know how much this tore me open. How much my heart bleeds from the loss of hope. Because that's all I had. One moment of realization followed by hours of hope he felt the same. That I wasn't out on a ledge by myself.

Turns out I was.

I nod once, turning from the anger etched deep into every line of his face and run for the door. Why couldn't this afternoon's events have happened in reverse? I turned down Jax because my heart was no longer in it. And now I'm left with nothing. Weeks of chasing him just to turn him down at a pivotal moment when it is clear he wanted me. *Me*. Not all the other skanks who would be at the party. Not even me in a pretty dress.

In a matter of ten minutes, I ruined not only my chances at an amazing summer with the guy I used to worship, but also a ten-year friendship. Scratch that. *Spencer* ruined our friendship the moment his lips touched mine. The moment he decided without my permission that he would make me fall just to leave me hanging.

Well, screw him.

Mumbling to myself, I march past a startled Ryan, and straight up the stairs. I'm going to that party tonight and I'm going to look so damn amazing Jax will have no choice but to forgive me.

And as for Spencer, well he can go screw himself.

A stupid rock catches the thin, sky-high heel of one of my boots and I stumble to the side, catching myself on a tree. I tug down the hem of my skirt, growling as I straighten and march down the dimly lit street toward the rows of cars and rumbling music. After having a couple of hours to calm down a bit, I've concluded this is the worst idea I've ever had.

Yet, it didn't stop me from throwing on a black leather skirt I knew was skimpy before buying and pairing it with a pair of knee-high boots I stole from my mom. At least the green off the shoulder top I have on is covering my torso and half of my arms. Still, I feel naked. Exposed. Or maybe that's my heart bleeding all over the place. With every step I take toward Jax it erodes. The damn thing has got to be black by now.

As I got dressed, I watched a moving truck come and four guys load up the entire house I practically grew up in. Then Spencer got into his car, not even sparing a glance in my direction and drove off after the truck.

So I added more black eyeliner and pulled my hair into a tight, scalp-tingling ponytail, and headed downstairs to catch my cab to the party.

I had the driver drop me off two blocks away, not wanting to draw attention. That's how I find myself walking alone in the dark in a pair of boots that could bust my ankle if I step wrong.

Ryan tried to question me as I left, but I blew him off. Part of my broken heart is owed to him. After all, he was the one who first hinted at Spencer and me as more than friends. On several occasions as a matter of fact. Had he kept his big mouth shut, I may never have been confused enough to let myself fall into such a terrible position.

Jax would have picked me up and we would be having a good time instead of wishing there were a few more streetlamps to light my way.

The music swells, growing louder as I make my way up the long drive. This house could not be on a bigger plot of land. I swear Malcolm's parents must own half the block.

Doubt creeps in was I climb the fifty freaking stairs to the front door and the few people outside shoot me curious, bordering on odd, looks. Yes, I'm aware I don't exactly fit in here. No amount of makeup and clothes with change seventeen years of being me. My stomach churns as I cross and uncross my arms, fighting the urge to pull down the skirt yet again.

Music rattles the windows and my bones before I step inside. The front door is open and from the porch where I hesitate, I can see bodies filling the living room and hallways. This is far rowdier than the party in the field. More claustrophobic.

I turn sideways and squeeze past a group hanging in front of the door and smack my elbow into a girl as one of her rowdy friends sways into me.

"Watch it!" she snaps, shooting me a stink-eye and

tugging the guy toward her as if I'm two seconds away from making a pass.

"Sorry." I rush past them farther into the house to a less crowded corner. From there I scan the faces of the many partygoers searching for Jax's wide frame.

I don't see him anywhere but spot Zoe and Haylee in the living room with a bunch of the guys from the football team.

Lord help me if I run into Will. He'll freak out and make a scene I'll never be able to recover from. No way in hell do I want to relive something like that for a whole school year.

I just need to find Jax. We can sneak off somewhere private or he can take me home because I forgot my phone and as I walk down the hallway toward the kitchen, I'm hit with how much I don't want to be here alone. Not with the way several guys have leered at me as I passed.

Where the hell is Jax?

I turn the corner into the kitchen and run smack-dab into someone.

"Sorry about that."

I glance up and up into the smiling face of a guy I don't recognize. He's got dark eyes, boarding on black and what my mom calls a Roman nose that's crooked as if it's been broken. His jaw flexes as his gaze drops lower to my bare thighs.

Letting out a nervous laugh, I step back as far as the tight space will allow.

"You look like you're on a mission," he drawls, dark eyes once again settling on my face.

"Was looking for someone."

"Got a name?"

"Um, someone from school." I search his face again but I don't recognize him. With a build like that, he's gotta play sports. And because of my brothers, I'm familiar with most of the guys on the team.

"Can I get you a drink?"

"No." Nerves clench my stomach and I glance around, but no one is paying attention to us. I don't know what it is, but this guy kind of icks me out. "I should go."

"But you just got here." His hand settles on my upper arm. "Let me get you a drink."

"No, it's—" My gaze slides past him into the corner of the kitchen in time to see Jax shove his tongue down the throat of some random girl. Awesome. So he's decided I'm not worth the trouble too.

The guy in front of me follows where I'm glaring. Realization dawns on his face and he nods. "Seems like you do need that drink now. Come on, legs, let's get you something to make you forget about tonight."

Forgetting. That's exactly what I need.

I follow him into the crowded kitchen keeping my back to Jax. He passes me a red plastic cup and I chug the bitter liquid before he's had the chance to pour himself one and without asking what it is.

His laughter rings out above the music. "My kind of girl." He passes me another cup, tipping his against it and we both knock them back.

A tiny voice in my head is screaming this isn't me. I don't drink. I don't party. And I sure as hell wouldn't be letting a guy I don't know run his hand down my arm and urge me on as he passes me a third drink. But I also wouldn't have kissed my best friend and changed who I was to score a guy who couldn't care less if I hung around. So maybe I don't know who I am. Maybe this *is* me.

I gulp down the liquid and smile as a warm sensation works its way through my stomach and mixes with the drunken flapping of butterflies. The guy smiles down at me and I realize I never caught his name.

"Rylee," I shout and point to my chest.

His smile grows and he mumbles out something that sounds like it doesn't matter and passes me another drink.

This time, it doesn't taste quite as bitter as the other three and the warm sensation turns almost numbing, helping me to block out my pain.

Perfect.

———

What feels like hours later, I stumble through the house as it spins around me in dizzying circles. Just like being on a Tilt-A-Whirl.

My new friend grips my waist as he maneuvers me through the crowded space toward a door and the fresh air I requested. Sweat drips down the back of my neck and I have to choke back the urge to vomit.

Cool air hits my face as I stumble out the door onto a pitch-black brick path. I glance around and in my distorted vision, I see there isn't anyone but us here. Closing my eyes, I tilt my head against the cold surface of the house and breathe in deep for the first time since arriving at the party.

Nothing has ever felt as good as standing outside in

the middle of the night. Except maybe when Spencer's lips were on mine.

Crap.

I was supposed to be forgetting about that jerk. It's not as if it will ever happen again. Might as well force him out of my mind and move on.

A warm hand on my cheek makes me crack my eyes open. Mystery Man stands in front of me, grinning from ear to ear as he stares down at me. He would kind of be cute if it weren't for the crooked teeth and all-around cocky manner about him.

"I need to get home," I mumble as he steps closer, forcing my body flat against the wall to keep space between us. Not a lie either. I'm fairly certain I'm past curfew. "Can you call me a cab?"

He shakes his head, the grin on his face never wavering even as his hands circle around my wrists and force them over my head. Even as I buck and slip sideways on the brick twisting my ankle. Not even as I say no and he crashes his mouth to mine and thrusts his tongue deep into my mouth almost choking me.

30

Spencer

Pounding on my front door rouses me from the crappy dream I was having. Though I'm pretty sure Rylee telling me to go screw myself is a lot better than what she'll really say to me when she finds out I didn't move to Washington but right up the road.

I stumble around the mess of boxes lining our new apartment living room and fling open the door expecting to see my mom who forgot her key when she went over to grab the last few items from the house. Instead, Ryan is standing there running an agitated hand through his hair.

"What's up?" I ask as he shoves his way inside.

"Where's Rylee?"

I flinch at the twisting in my gut at the mere mention of her name. "No clue. Maybe she's with her boyfriend."

"She's not here?" Ryan's eyes go wide and he curses, reaching inside his pocket for his phone.

"Like I said, she's probably with Jax."

Ryan pauses what he's doing to throw a glare almost as good as Rylee's my way. "She's not with Jax."

Sure looked that way this afternoon.

"I'm telling you she—"

"And I'm telling you she's not!" Ryan snaps.

Fear floods every vein in my body and I have to

swallow down the lump in my throat just to speak. "What's going on?"

"She left a little after eight dressed like some chick from a rap video. Wouldn't tell me where she was going and now I can't get ahold of her. It's past curfew. She's never late."

"What are you saying?"

"I'm saying we need to find her before my parents get home."

"Where's Will?" Unease grows in my stomach rooting me to the floor even though Ryan hasn't stopped pacing. Normally, I wouldn't be too concerned. So she's not home on a Saturday night, who cares? But Ryan is showing an uncharacteristic amount of concern, which has me thrown.

"He's checking the skate park." Ryan glares at the screen of his phone. "Do you know of any parties tonight?"

I shake my head, sucking my bottom lip between my teeth so hard I'm surprised it's not bleeding. Ryan grips the phone in a fist and looks as if he's seconds away from throwing it across the room. That's when I notice the case. Rylee's case.

"Is that her phone?"

"Yeah. She left it. Found that out forty minutes ago when I called it."

"Here." I motion for him to hand it over with frantic fingers. Once it's in my hands I type in her password and click on her text messages.

"How do you know her password? I've been trying to figure it out all night."

I roll my eyes and throw him a withering look. Then I

do the one thing I never wanted to do and click on the text chain from Jax. To my relief, there isn't anything new for almost a week. Relieve turns sour in my stomach because that means his stop by her house wasn't planned.

"Anything?" Ryan asks.

"No."

I go to lock the phone when a thought so disgusting I almost ignore it pops into my head. It's the last thing I would ever want to do but if Rylee is in trouble somewhere and I didn't do everything in my power to help her, I wouldn't be able to live with myself.

I click back into her texts and type out a nauseating message.

"Sexy?" Ryan grumbles over my shoulder.

"I'm grasping at straws here." I hit Send and together we wait, both pacing a hole in the floor for the ten minutes it takes for Jax to respond.

"What does it say?" Ryan asks, grabbing for the phone.

"It says she should have taken him up on his invite earlier. Now he's got a better offer." I growl in frustration as Ryan snatches the phone from me.

"Let's give him some motivation then." He types in a response that will have Rylee kicking his butt when she finds out.

"She's going to kill you."

"Whatever." Ryan grins as Jax's response comes through almost instantly. "He's at Malcolm's. I'm assuming that's where she went."

"But he hasn't seen her, clearly."

"You got a better idea?" Ryan throws over his shoulder as he bolts out the front door.

No. No, I don't. So I follow him out and down the stairs to where his car is waiting. We better find her there, because I'm facing my own curfew violation and a month grounding if we're caught.

———

Fifteen minutes later Ryan pulls up outside of Malcolm's house.

"It will take forever to find a parking spot." I scan the road but there's nothing. Not even up his long driveway.

"You go. I'll find a spot."

I hop out and run up the lawn as Ryan peels out and flips around. Ducking past a group of kids from homeroom on the porch, I fly into the house and scan the crowd. It's so damn crowded I can only make it in a couple of inches so I resort to height, searching for a mess of brown hair that sticks up above the rest.

"What are you doing here?" I spin around as Zoe makes her way over to me, swinging her hips so hard I'm surprised she's staying upright. "I don't remember you getting an invite. Not after how you treated me."

"Have you seen Rylee?" I ask, scanning the hallway behind her.

"Rylee Everett?" She examines her nails not even bothering to fake interest in the conversation. "She was here earlier in the most ridiculous outfit. Desperation never looks good on anyone."

My glare is sharp enough to at least break through her bitchy attitude for the briefest of seconds. "Where did she go?"

"My guess is she bounced when Jax wouldn't give her

the time of day. Last I saw she was making a fool of herself in the kitchen."

"When was that?"

"About five minutes ago."

I don't wait for her to say any more. I race into the kitchen knocking into a few people in the process, ignoring the cursing and threats on my life.

She's nowhere to be found.

But there's Jax in the corner with his tongue so far down a girl's throat I'm surprised she hasn't suffocated.

My heart starts to race and I grip the wall to keep myself upright. This isn't her. She would never put herself in a position like this. So where the hell is she? My gut tells me she bolted after seeing the guy she's been after for years going at it without a care in the world. If that was the case though she would be home. Safe.

I notice a door to the backyard on the fall wall and push my way to it. When I stumble outside there are three guys hovering by a fire pit not far from the porch. I take a deep breath, reveling in the silence for one heart-beat before I hear it.

"Stop," Rylee whimpers.

Her words are followed by grunting and what sounds like a solid hit against a face. Through the fear and rage clouding my vision, I round the corner and I can just barely make out Rylee sitting on the ground with her head propped against the wall. Her short skirt is pushed dangerously high. At her feet, Ryan has a guy pinned beneath him and is landing blow after blow to the guy's face as he tries to block and throw him off.

I run over to her, gripping under her arms and pulling her up. She lets out a sigh as her shaking arms wrap around my middle. Her shirt is torn on one shoulder, dropping down to reveal her black bra. Her makeup is smeared and her eyes are glassy. She looks nothing like my Rylee.

I'm going to kill this guy.

"Spence..."

"Shh." My hand trails down her back as the other yanks down the hem of her skirt. A sickening gut feeling tells me what almost happened and rage boils through my veins in a way I've never felt before.

If Ryan wasn't in the middle of an epic smackdown I would beg for a turn. Whoever this guy is deserves a brutal lesson in keeping his hands off things that don't belong to him.

"Are you okay...did he?"

She shakes her head, burying her tear-stained face into my chest. That's all I need to know. I can't handle hearing anything else.

"Stay the hell away from my sister!" Ryan spits, as he climbs off the guy, wiping blood from under his nose where he must have taken a shot to the face. The only shot judging from the condition of the guy groaning on the ground. "And the next time a girl says no, you listen."

The guy moans, curling into a ball as I scoop Rylee into my arms. I don't care about her weak protests or the fact that a small group has gathered to watch the fight. All I care about is getting her to Ryan's car and back to the safety of her house.

None of this would have happened if I had stayed calm this afternoon. If I didn't push her away and lie about where I was moving to. She would be at home right now, no doubt with me by her side as we eat our weight in pizza and watch her favorite movie for the thousandth time.

Instead, I was a selfish, vengeful prick.

"What happened?" I ask once we reach the street and I'm positive the guy or his friends won't be coming after us.

Ryan's still running off adrenaline, physically vibrating at my side. "He had his hands all over her, man. She was saying no, and he didn't stop. If we hadn't gotten here when we did..."

Swallowing past what feels like razor blades I glance down at her face all squished against my heaving chest. The mere thought of him touching her makes me want to go back and break every bone in his freaking hands so he can never lay a finger on another person.

Ryan props open the passenger door and shoves the seat forward giving me room to set Rylee down. When my hands leave her back, she reaches out for me whimpering.

"God, I love you," she mumbles and then vomits all over the sidewalk and my shoes before passing out.

Ryan laughs for the first time tonight as he rounds the car. "Knew it," he says, then slams his door leaving me alone in silence.

She loves me?

A grin forms on my lips as I climb into the car. I would have preferred to hear those words from her sober and not seconds before vomiting on my shoes.

But hell, I'll take them any time and any way I can.

31
Rylee

My head pounds in time with my heart. Moving my head to the side to find the time was enough to make me want to vomit.

Something I did at least once last night judging from my hair.

Not to get into too many details, but let's just say there was a bit of physical evidence.

I run a clammy palm over my forehead and wish for death. It has to be better than how I feel this very moment.

"Good morning, sunshine." Ryan pops his head into my room and I flip him the bird, rolling over.

I have no clue how I got home—or really anything after the fourth drink—but I'm pretty sure Ryan played a part. I definitely remember seeing a beat-up yellow Mustang.

"Told Mom you started yacking after eating sushi. She bought it for now, but I would get up and at least brush your teeth. Unless you want her to find out you drank the football team under the table."

"Go away." My lips crack from the movement, stinging as I run my dry tongue over them.

"I'm serious. You need to get up." His weight hits the bed, bouncing me and I once again cover my mouth and force down the urge to puke. "At least drink some water." He shoves a water bottle in my direction.

When I focus on him I gasp and rear back making my head pound again. "What happened to your face?"

His grin is fleeting as he shakes his head. "You don't remember?"

I remember not thinking anything through when I went to the party. Once I got there, it was clear Jax never cared about me and most likely saw our relationship—if it can even be called that—as another conquest.

Then alcohol.

Lots and lots of alcohol.

"What did you do?" I ask as so many scenarios of my brother going full-out protector mode and embarrassing me in front of half the school flashes through my mind.

"Beat the crap out of some guy who got handsy. You're lucky Will was off searching for you at the skate park."

Small snips of the party crash in. A strange guy. Red cups. Night air. Creepy hands roaming all over my body. There's even a glimpse of Spencer but that makes no sense because he should have been on his way to Washington.

"Now, if you weren't so hung over, I would make you pay for making me show the school how much I care about my baby sister."

"By three minutes," I mumble, which gains a smile.

"Just know there will be revenge." He pats my ankle as he stands. "When you least expect it," he throws over his shoulder and shuts the door.

I groan and roll over, smashing my face in the pillows. No way I can deal with any of this right now.

So I go back to sleep and pray I don't resemble death when I wake.

———

My mom wakes me sometimes before dinner. A look of pure concern washes over her face when she sees me and I know if I don't at least try to eat, she'll make me go to the doctor.

So I get up.

And wish again for death.

I'm never drinking again.

I trail her downstairs, throwing my hair into a messy bun to hide how gross it is. I'm just thankful my dad is at some team-building thing for work today because he can spot a hangover. I do have two older brothers after all. Mom prefers to remain oblivious. Something I'm so very thankful for at the moment.

"It lives," Ryan mocks as I hit the bottom step.

"Be nice to your sister. She's under the weather."

"Uh-huh." Will gives me a nasty glare as he walks into the kitchen.

So, he knows about my drunken escapades. Awesome.

"You're going to wish you listened to me about brushing your teeth," Ryan sings as he catches up to Will.

It's not until I follow him into the kitchen that I realize what he meant. Because there sits my best friend who should be in Washington according to the quick mapping I did before the party.

Yet, here he is in his same old chair with an expression bouncing between amused and annoyed.

"You really should check your phone," he says as he accepts a soda from my mom with a quick smile.

Okay, true. But to be fair I have no idea where it's at. Haven't seen it since before the party.

"Oh, right." Ryan slides my phone across the table to me and shares a grin with Spencer that raises all the hairs on my arms.

Something super strange is going on here.

I go to check and make sure they didn't put it in another language or sext everyone in my contacts, but Mom clucks her tongue putting an end to that idea. No phone at the table. One of the most hated rules in our house.

Spencer hands me 7-Up. "Here, I know you *love* this when you're sick."

Ryan snickers and snags a piece of bread from the wicker basket in the middle of the table. "Don't you *love* garlic bread too?"

This gains a laugh from both of them and I can tell Will is trying hard to hold on to his frown.

What the hell is going on?

Seriously, the only person at the table not acting like a total weirdo is my mom.

"Yeah...they're okay I guess." I take a sip of water and send up a silent *thank you* to the man above when it stays down. I turn my attention to the boy next to me. "Shouldn't you be in Washington?"

"Yeah, but he *loved* it here too much to leave," Ryan says and then howls with laughter causing Spencer to cover his mouth to hold composure.

Across the table, Will cracks and shakes his head.

What in the freaking hell is going on with these three?

"Boys," Mom admonishes and starts dishing out pieces of fried chicken. "How was the move, Spencer?"

"Good, Mrs. Everett. Just unpacking now."

"How are you here?" I ask, then gag when chicken is passed in front of my face.

"Called a car, dumb a—"

"Ryan!" Mom's face turns a bright shade of red. A color I swear only Ryan can bring her to.

Ryan takes a bite out of the crispy thigh Mom passed him and oil dribbles down his chin.

So, I guess he's over being the sweet version of himself. If I were feeling better, his lap would be covered in mashed potatoes and I would be forced to clean the whole house as punishment. Which, all things considered, is a small price to pay.

"Can we please just have a nice dinner?" Mom asks.

In response there is a chorus of, "Yes, ma'am." Followed by, "Yes, Mrs. Everett." Then the table falls quiet as silverware on plates rings out.

I, on the other hand, can't stomach anything so I sit back and watch as Ryan shoots Spencer odd looks I can't interpret. Will even jumps in a few times. By the time everyone is done and Will is cleaning off the table, I'm seconds away from screaming.

How on Earth—or more accurately—what on Earth, happened from the time Spencer moved and the party last night?

Maybe it's because I'm a little shaken from seeing him at my table when he should be several states away that I'm not angrier. Relief is the primary emotion running through my bones. Relief and fear because we still haven't talked about the kiss. A kiss I haven't been able to purge from my mind. Not even with copious amounts of alcohol swimming through my system.

Is that why I hallucinated Spencer being with Ryan?

"Hey." His thigh bumps mine as he stands. "Want to go outside and talk?"

"She'd *love* to," Ryan chimes in as he rocks back in his chair.

I take Spencer's outstretched hand then drop it and step away the second Ryan burst out laughing.

"Come on." He motions toward the front door and I follow, shooting one more glare over my shoulder at my two brothers who can't hide their grins.

Spencer plops down on the porch swing and pats the spot next to him. When I hesitate, he sighs and latches on to my wrist tugging until I land in the spot right next to him. So close, in fact, I can smell his deodorant and feel the heat from his legs on mine.

"So..." My hands twist in my lap but I refuse to focus on him, instead I stare at the house across the street sitting empty and sad without his car in the driveway.

"I didn't move to Washington."

"I kinda gathered that."

"But I did move."

"Figured that out too."

Spencer reaches out and grips my chin, tugging toward him until my gaze meets his. "My parents sold the house and my mom got an apartment down the street so I could finish my senior year here."

When I don't say anything Spencer's eyes soften the way they do when he's trying to be gentle with my feelings. My muscles tense, waiting for him to tell me what a mistake that kiss was. Instead, he slips a hand into my hair and cups the back of my head tugging me toward him.

"What you did last night was stupid. No one knew where you were. You didn't bring your phone. Anything could have happened."

I wince and focus on my lap.

"The Rylee I know never would have put herself in that position. Hell, she never would have changed everything that made her awesome just to land some loser."

"You're right." As much as I hate to admit it, he is. I went eight shades of crazy the past few weeks chasing what I now know is some exaggerated fantasy. Jax Lever isn't all he's cracked up to be.

But my actions last night...Well, those were all due to Spencer. When I thought he was leaving I cracked and turned into someone I didn't recognize.

After a few minutes of silence Spencer's hand lands on mine. "Do you have anything you want to tell me?" he asks, his stupid full lips tipping up at the corners. "Pretend we're underwater. Tell me a secret."

"I'm never going to drink again."

Laughter tips his head back. "Kinda figured that after you puked all over my shoes."

I cringe, trying to pull away but he doesn't let me. "The state fair all over again."

"Except it wasn't pink." When his gaze locks on mine, my lungs stop working. "And I'm pretty sure you said you hated me while you were puking your guts out at the state fair. You had a different sentiment last night."

I gasp as flashes of the night trickle in. None of them

are in order and most don't make any sense, but one moment sitting in Ryan's car sticks. Now their annoying banter at the table makes sense.

Please God, tell me I didn't blurt out my feelings last night.

The way Spencer is smiling tells me I might have.

"So, you lied to me about moving. Why?" I change the subject. It's the only thing I can think of to get myself out of having to explain how I was stupid enough to go and fall for him.

"Because I saw you kissing Jax, and it pissed me off. When you said you love me did you mean it as more than your best friend?"

Dang it.

My mouth drops open and nothing comes out. What the hell do I say to that? *Oh, hey. Yeah after almost ten years I've discovered I'm madly in love with you and would kill for a chance to have your lips on mine again.* If that's not creepy I don't know what is.

"Rylee?"

I shake my head and try to pull away. I can't do this. I can't say it knowing I'll never be able to take it back now that I'm sober.

Spencer's hand tightens and he tugs me forward until our foreheads touch. "Did you mean what you said or was it the whole white knight moment?"

"I..."

"Because I love you. And I don't mean as my best friend, although that's mixed in there. I mean it as the girl of my dreams who I can't get over no matter how hard I try. That kiss only screwed me further and believe me when I say I almost murdered Jax when I saw his lips on yours because the only person who should be kissing you is me. Only me."

His lips brush against mine and I gasp at the sensation shooting through every limb.

"I have a hunch you feel the same way but I need to hear it." His thumb tugs down on my bottom lip freeing it from the tight grip of my teeth. "I need you to say the words out loud so I can stop thinking I'm crazy."

"I..."

This is it. Sink or swim. Run or stay.

When I look into his eyes all apprehension melts away and all I can see is him. Us. Our future. And I hate myself for all the time I wasted before I realized.

I'm in love with my best friend.

"I love you so much I'm not going to kill you for lying about moving to another state."

His smile is so wide it crinkles the corners of his eyes, making them sparkle the way they always do when he's truly happy.

"Scratch that. I love you so much I would let you pick any movie you wanted every single Saturday for the rest of our lives."

His breath hits my mouth as he laughs. "And I love you enough to kiss you even though I know you probably haven't brushed your teeth since last night." The next second his lips are on mine.

This is the only place I ever want to be.

Epilogue
Spencer

Music pumps out of the sound system Will moved outside on to the deck. Mr. Everett stands at the grill flipping burgers as kids hang out around him laughing and enjoying the feeling of being released from high school. Pretty much every newly graduated senior except one.

Will threatened to end Jax's life when he saw him the Monday after the party. He still blames him for Rylee putting herself into that situation. Who he should blame is me, but I sure as hell won't be telling him. On the plus side, Jax hasn't so much as glanced her way the past month.

Now he'll be out of my life for good.

I glance over to the far end of the backyard where Zoe stands with Micky Donaldson. She sends me a wink and turns her attention to him, laughing at whatever he said.

According to the few passing conversations we've had, they plan on moving in together in an off-campus apartment in the fall. A tad bit quick if you ask me, but who am I to judge? Took me way too long to admit how I felt about Rylee. And if I didn't think her brothers would murder me and hide my body where no one would find it, I would jump at the opportunity to live with her when we head off to college next summer.

Because the truth is, I'm exactly where I want to be. Nothing could change it. Not even being forced to complete the stupid challenge I've been putting off for months.

Earlier today Rylee and I completed our dare and jumped into the school swimming pool wearing our nicest clothes. Then we joined her family at Will's graduation ceremony. I'll never forget the initial look of shock on her mom's face that morphed into a smile when we sat down next to her sopping wet and holding hands. Happy would be an understatement when she found out we were dating. My hunch is she's already planning our wedding. Which she might have an easier time doing since my girl has embraced her girly side.

Not all the time and definitely not at the skate park. But she knows how to turn it on when she wants to.

Arms wrap around me from behind and I twist to see Rylee smiling up at me. "Think anyone would notice if we snuck out of here and headed back to your apartment?"

I spin her around until her chest is pressed against mine. "Probably. 'Rents are on high alert now that they know we're together. No more sleepovers in the same bed."

"I told you we should hide it from them."

"Kind of hard what with your evil twin having a giant mouth."

He caught us kissing on the porch the afternoon when we grew a pair and admitted our feelings. Took him all of five seconds to alert the entire house. Even called Noah whose response was a quick *told you so* before hanging up.

"Hey."

We twist to see Will marching toward us with Ryan

bouncing around at his side from the three energy drinks he's inhaled.

"Will," Rylee growls, a warning clear in her voice.

Will holds up his hands. "Just want to talk to him for a quick second. Why don't you go help Mom in the kitchen?"

Her eyes narrow as she steps away. "That was bordering on sexist and you're lucky your friends are here and Mom told me to be on my best behavior."

She rolls her eyes and stretches up to plant a kiss on my cheek. It's a compromise because her brothers made it clear if they catch us making out she will be down a best friend and boyfriend.

Once she's inside the house, Will crosses his arms and turns to me. "You will not hurt my sister. No parties. No drinking. Hands stay off everything from the shoulders down." He steps forward, a hand squeezing my shoulder for emphasis. In the next second, his fist hits my stomach hard enough to hunch me over as I gasp for air. "Just a warning."

Ryan laughs as Will walks away toward a group of friends. "Sorry, bro. She's still our sister." He pats my head and follows his brother, throwing a grin my way before he scoops up Christy, the girl he's currently seeing and spins her around.

"Will give you the big brother speech?" Rylee asks.

"Yup." I grip my stomach as I stand. "I'm not allowed to touch anything south of your shoulders."

"Then don't tell him about last night." Her grin is wicked as she steps into me, not caring that her brothers are standing watch. "And definitely don't tell him about how you're going to sneak out of Noah's old room after everyone goes to bed."

"You trying to get me killed?" I wrap her in my arms and tug until she's pressed against me right where I like her.

"Why would I do that when I haven't had nearly enough time with you as my boyfriend?"

My eyebrows jump and I lean back. "Boyfriend, huh? Thought you didn't want to put labels on this yet."

"Come on, Hendricks. I was being a chickenshit. Besides, there's no way in hell I want these chicks getting ideas about you being on the market."

"No longer single and ready to mingle?"

"Not as long as I have a say in it. You dropped the *L* word so you're stuck with me now."

"I can live with that." I kiss the tip of her nose and she smiles. "By the way, I like the dressy grunge thing you got going on. How did your mom react to the fishnet?"

She shrugs. "It was her idea. I'll never get used to this new ground we've settled on. I swear, it's rubbing off on her." She motions to her mom who is busy setting paper plates and plastic silverware on the table.

No lie. I don't think I've ever seen her in a pair of ripped jeans let alone a flannel shirt. "Did we fall into some crazy episode of *The Twilight Zone*?"

"If we did, I never want to leave." She links her hands behind my neck. "So. We have the whole summer ahead of us."

"We do. You still up for a trip to Oregon State?"

She pulls a funny face and winces. "Now that you've told the world how much you love me, I bet my parents won't be too keen on letting me take a weekend trip alone with you."

"We could always—"

"Don't say the evil twin."

"Well, you turn eighteen in a month."

She gasps, her eyes going wide in mock horror. "You're right. Then I'll be the adult in this relationship. Might as well get all the kissing in now before I'm a cradle robber."

I grab her sides and she laughs. "For three weeks. Then we're both eighteen and free to do whatever we want."

"Yeah, 'cause my parents will go for that argument."

"Guess you have no choice but to include Ryan."

She sighs and tips her head back. "I was afraid of that."

"So, tell me, girlfriend. What do you want to do with the rest of the night?"

She grins and peeks over my shoulder where everyone is lining up to grab food. "I hear there's a crazy boring movie that just came out." When my eyebrows crumple in confusion hers jump. "I can think of a few things we could do. Alone. In a dark theater."

I grab her hand and yank her toward the gate while she laughs and shouts that we're going to the movies.

"This is going to be a great summer," I whisper into her hair before planting a kiss under her ear, making her shiver. "Maybe I'll even show you a few things on that cute little board of yours."

Rylee breaks from my grasp and spins around. "You're so on, Hendricks."

I can't help but smile at the fire in her eyes. What

started out as a crappy year is turning out better than I ever could have imagined.

After all, I managed to snag the girl of my dreams. It just so happens she's also my best friend.

And who could ask for more than that?

ABOUT THE AUTHOR

A.R. Perry is an American-born author who has lived all over the US due to her wanderlust husband. She has a degree in photography and massage therapy yet somehow works in human resources.

When she's not working, reading, or writing she can be found sleeping because the day is practically done. Thank goodness for coffee, chocolate, and Panic! At The Disco or nothing would ever get done.

The Dating Dare

Heartbreak Café

Melt My Heart

Popularity is Just an Equation

Made in the USA
Columbia, SC
26 May 2020

98386378R00145